Geoff Dean left school at age 16 for an apprenticeship with a house-painting firm. He was sacked for writing rude words on the brick wall he was supposed to be painting. He was also sacked from his next job as cashier in a travelling side-show act (The Wall of Death) when it was found he couldn't do arithmetic. Since then he has been a carpenter, window-dresser, tourist guide and ticket writer in Australia, a lumberjack and fisherman in Canada, and a sewing machine salesman in Britain. His longest full-time job, other than writing, was a fourteen year stint as dairy farmer and pig farmer in Tasmania.

Geoff Dean has published four books of short stories. His latest, *The Hadlee Stories*, is also published by Esperance Press.

"Geoff Dean is an accomplished writer of short stories with a fine reputation in Australia. His collection of stories, Over the Fence, contains his best work and I've admired these stories for over a decade. Australian Short Stories magazine has published a number of Dean's stories over the past 15 years and we consider him to be amongst the best storytellers in the country."

Bruce Pascoe
Australian Short Stories

"These simple yarns build to unexpected conclusions ... Dean's characters emerge fully-formed and unique. His deft descriptions and pithy dialogue are economical and highly amusing."

Giles Hugo
The Mercury, Hobart

... You could always expect Elsa to say or do the unexpected.

Published with the assistance of the
Minister for the Arts, Sport and Recreation
through ARTS TASMANIA

and with thanks to Elizabeth Dean who related the original versions of some of these stories to the author.

ISBN 1 876342 02 1

Copyright Geoff Dean 1998

All rights reserved. No part of this publication may be reproduced, stored in a retrieval system, or transmitted, in any form or by any means, electronic, mechanical, photocopying, recording or otherwise, without the prior permission of the publishers

Published by
Esperance Press
as part of the series *Writers of the Huon*
Editor: Edith Speers
Illustrations: Stephen Pile
Book Design & Cover Design:
Edith Speers

Dover, Tasmania, Australia 7117
Ph (03) 62981552 Fax (03) 62981197
dovertc@tassie.net.au
http://www.tassie.net.au/esperance.press

Tasmanian Bush Yarns

OVER THE FENCE

Geoff Dean

For Caroline, Benjamin and Annabel

Contents

Author's Introduction	1
Rolly's Special Remedy	3
The Amazing Resurrection of Grandma Pike	13
The Year of the Cherry	21
Willum and the Tax Men	27
The Biggest Cray in the World	33
The Chocolate Pigs	41
Three Birds with One Stone	49
Finders Keepers	57
A Favour Given is a Favour Returned	63
A Private Kind of Humour	71
Bonfire Night	81
Flash	87
A Taste of Pig	93
The Devils, the Butcher, and the Rotary Barbecue	101
Christmas Goose	113
The Much Travelled Boar	119
The Uncertain Burial of Elsa Gernhart	127
Whisky Wedding	137
Nothing But the Best	151
Scorpio Rising	159
Dear Editor	169
Bert Morley's Killing	177

Author's Introduction

The main aim of this book is to re-introduce readers to the art of the laconic country story. It is an art which I consider is sadly lacking in current Australian writing, but fortunately not in the psyche of the average Aussies who tell stories like these in every country town I've ever known.

I do not make the claim that these stories are wholly factual, although one way or another, the majority are in part based on fact. For example, "The Uncertain Burial of Elsa Gernhart" was constructed around a true incident that occurred at a makeshift funeral in the Fingal Valley in the thirties. "The Year of the Cherry" was also developed from an actual occurrence.

Yarns such as "Flash" and "The Much Travelled Boar" were, give or take a certain amount of embroidery, drawn from personal experience when my family and I were farming in the north-east of Tasmania in the nineteen-sixties. Other stories were related to me over fences, over cups of tea at kitchen tables, in potato paddocks, in hay barns, in pubs on wet afternoons. In most cases the narrator offered to swear "on a stack of Bibles too big to shake a stick at" that the story was true.

However later, having heard various versions of the same yarn involving more often than not a whole new set of protagonists, I came to the conclusion that it wasn't so much a matter of the truth as it was an innate human desire to tell a story and put one's individual stamp on it. This seems especially so with country people and in the case of this book, with me.

Neither do you ever, as the saying goes, stuff up a good story for the want of a few facts. Which is another version, I suggest, of that much maligned Australian attitude expressed in the phrase "she'll be right, mate." In my opinion this is not so much a matter of laziness or carelessness as it is of innovation. Making do with what you've got. The equivalent of using baling wire (or twine) to fix whatever needs fixing when nothing else is available.

It is, I think, the essence of Australian-ness which when translated into humour becomes more of a wry grin than a belly laugh. A kind of humour that has grown out of the conflict between the Australian settler and the unrelenting landscape. If the human element in this conflict is not prepared to bend a bit - to make the best of things as they are - to laugh even when the chips are down - then something will break and it won't be the land. So the humour in the end is not so much a matter of jollity as it is of retrieving the best out of a bad situation. "Yeah mate, I broke me leg, but only at the small end."

With this book I have endeavoured to capture that unique quality of humour.

Rolly's Special Remedy

Rolly Hills was Montvale district's unofficial stock agent who operated out of his two hectare property on the outskirts of the town. There were more sheds on Rolly's small property than the average fully operational farm, and every shed was chock-o-block full of something. Old machinery, blacksmith's paraphernalia, horse boxes, buggies, trailers, fodder - even old pieces of furniture in various stages of disrepair. You name it and you were likely to find it in one of Rolly's sheds.

And that wasn't to mention the livestock. Fowls of all colours and ages, geese, ducks, cats and dogs had set up camp in one shed or another. Entering any of these sheds day or night usually brought on a squall of activity. A blizzard of feathers and fur flew all around as the shed's various occupants either scattered before the invader or romped ecstatically at their feet.

You could also usually depend on a few sheep, a goat or two and some pigs of various ages to be picking their way around the sparse grass in one or other of the small paddocks. More than likely there would be an old horse to be seen, too, either leaning against the wall of one of the rickety old sheds sheltering from the wind, or standing quietly in the shade of the one and only eucalypt tree that grew on the property.

Yet for all that, there was also a transitory sense about the place because even though you could rely on something being there, you couldn't always rely on it being the same as it was the week before. One week the old horse would be a half-draught and the next week a spindly-looking racer, due for the knackers' yard. The goats seemed to change colour and gender overnight. Even the heaped piles of shit-encrusted furniture rarely remained for more than a few days at a time before they mysteriously disappeared and were replaced by a slightly different but equally dilapidated lot.

In his late forties Rolly was a fine specimen of country manhood. He was deep-voiced, barrel-chested, broad-shouldered and well over six feet tall with a head of hair birds might like to nest in. But his physical solidness wasn't his greatest asset. His greatest asset was his unassailable optimism which, combined with his unfailing wit, made him a force to be reckoned with in the world of buying and selling - an occupation, incidentally, that Rolly treated as others might treat a religion.

It was said in the district that Rolly would rather make a bad deal than no deal at all. But the real story was he rarely made a bad deal anyway. He had a prodigious memory and eyes and ears that missed nothing. Nine times out of ten if he didn't have something someone wanted he knew just where he could get it. Anything you could name from a bag of spuds to a bulldozer. However, for some unstated reason, Rolly's first love was buying and selling bulls. He was a kind of specialist in bulls and his ability to handle them nothing short of uncanny. Even the wildest, most wayward fence breaker, would wilt under his eyeball to eyeball gaze and become docile enough to be kidded into his horse box for a ride somewhere or other.

If for any reason a farmer in the District suddenly found himself short of a bull at mating time, Rolly would get to hear about it. Within an hour or two he'd be on their doorstep. "Need a bull, urgent, matey? No worries, I know just where I can get just what you want, an' it'll cost yer a whole heap less than any of those so-called stud breeders ud charge."

Rolly's gung-ho method of dealing in bulls had worked quite well for several years, but after Cec Jones' recently purchased, bargain-priced, "pure-bred" Angus bull had begun throwing multi-coloured calves, and Denny Bourke's "pedigree" Jersey developed a curious interest in Denny's beef steers rather than his prime dairy heifers, Rolly's clientele were inclined to become a mite more wary.

There wasn't a lot of learning in the district - at best a Grade 8 education, but that didn't mean those who lived there were thick. It only meant that they had to substitute their lack of formal education with something else, and what better way to do it than to learn the hard way, from direct and painful experience.

And thus, having once suffered one's own calamity, it was necessary to invent a maxim, as both a reminder to one's self and a warning to one's compatriots. A few well chosen words that told the story as directly and succinctly as possible. In Rolly's case the maxim read: "In

There were more sheds on Rolly's small property than the average fully operational farm ...

matters of livestock it was okay to sell to Rolly if the price was right but never buy from him no matter what the price."

Nevertheless, it should be said that Rolly did involve himself in the occasional legitimate transaction. And ironically it was one such transaction that almost backfired on him. So much so that he had to draw on the deepest reservoir of his almost legendary wit to save the day and come out, if not on top, at least Even Stevens.

The case in point was the time Colonel Foote's much valued and ancient Hereford bull collapsed suddenly halfway through the season. The huge beast just lay down one morning and refused to get up. He was coaxed by the Colonel's foreman with the very best clover hay, and enticed by the best looking and bull-hungry in-season heifers in the Colonel's herd, but it did no good. The animal just lay there in the house paddock contemplating his final resting place with the same kind of grim determination that had once made him the pride of the Colonel's bull-pen.

Not even two massive injections from Russ Chalmers the vet made poor old Caesar blink, let alone stagger to his feet and continue on the legitimate task he was born for. "I guess he's had it," Russ told the Colonel. "You may as well shoot him and bury the old bugger right where he is."

But the Colonel wasn't the sort of man who let sentiment for an old favourite stand in the way of making himself a bob or two. He rang Rolly Hills. "Poor old Caesar's gone down," he told Rolly. "He's the best bull I ever had but there's just no moving him. He's ready for the knackers I'm afraid. You can have him for forty dollars if you want."

"C'mon now Colonel," Rolly replied. "If yer can't move him, what good's he to me?"

"Yes, I take your point, Mr Hills," the Colonel said. "I guess I'll just have to take the vet's advice and shoot him then."

"Well," said Rolly, "if yer only goin' to shoot him yer might just as well give him to me an' save yerself the trouble of buryin' him. I could cut him up right where he lies an' take him off your hands."

Now the Colonel was far and away the biggest and richest land holder in the district but he had his pride to consider. He didn't want it said that he had given Rolly Hills something for nothing, so he compromised. "Okay," he said eventually, "I'll let you have him for twenty dollars on the proviso he is off my property one way or another by this evening."

The story has it that Rolly arrived at the Colonel's place with his horse box in tow inside seven minutes, and he had to hitch up and drive two miles in that time.

The Colonel heard him drive past his house towards the bull paddock while he was having his morning break and he hadn't even finished his second cup of tea before Rolly arrived on his door step with the twenty dollar note in his hand. The Colonel couldn't believe his eyes. The bull was actually standing up in Rolly's horse box, glaring all around in a glazed and puzzled way as if he had been tricked into something but wasn't sure how or what.

"How in the hell did you do it, man?" he asked Rolly.

Rolly just winked and passed the Colonel the twenty dollar note. "My special remedy, Colonel," was all he offered.

The Colonel shrugged. "Well, I guess a deal's a deal. I suppose you'll take the poor old feller to the knackers' yards for dog meat, hey?"

Rolly's face was expressionless. "Not on yer life, Colonel, a good sound bull like this'll be worth a packet at the abattoirs."

Without another word Rolly hopped back in his ute and drove off leaving the Colonel metaphorically nailed to his doorstep; and if anyone had been there to witness the event they couldn't have failed to notice that the Colonel's face was adorned with the same glazed expression that his once favourite bull had displayed a few seconds earlier...

But it also has to be told that Rolly didn't get it all his own way that day because in a small town not twenty miles down the road towards the abattoir he was stopped by the police doing a spot road check. Because of the hard times around the country there had been a fair bit of cattle duffing going on in recent months and the police were trying to put a stop to it.

The sergeant in charge recognised Rolly's ute and box trailer, and even though he considered Rolly was too smart an operator to be caught duffing in broad daylight, he thought it worth while giving his favourite enemy a bit of a tug. He stepped forward and flagged Rolly down.

"What have we got today, Mr Hills?" he asked through the open passenger's window.

Unfortunately for Rolly the bull by this time had come to the conclusion that whatever trick had been played on him wasn't to his liking at all. Head down and rear legs lashing out, old Caesar seemed bent on turning Rolly's box trailer into a heap of junk.

"Fair go, sergeant," Rolly said as he glanced anxiously through the rear window towards the precariously swaying trailer. "You know me Sarge. Give us a break."

In fact the reason that the sergeant had stopped Rolly in the first place was because he did know him. And in this case he interpreted Rolly's rather anxious manner as a possible sign of guilt. He resolved to turn Rolly over good and proper. He walked slowly around the back of the shuddering trailer then back up to the driver's side of the ute where he could see the bull's head tossing about through the iron grill. His own slow head-shaking seemed to indicate a certain amount of respect for the bull inside.

"A pretty fierce sort of bull you got there, Rolly," he said finally. "Where might you have got such a fine lookin' beast as that from?"

"Colonel Foote," Rolly said. "You can check if yer like. He sold the bull to me this morning. I'm takin' him to the abattoirs, ain't I."

"Seems like a pretty good bull to be taken to the abattoirs wouldn't you say, Rolly?"

By now Rolly was beginning to get a little desperate. "Look," he told the sergeant, "if I don't git goin' pretty soon that bull's gonner kick its way out and take to the bush."

But the sergeant wasn't going to be hurried. He had his job to do. "Well, Rolly, you know how it is. We have to check now don't we? Not that we don't believe you, of course. Perhaps you got a receipt of sale?"

Rolly groaned. "No, I din't get a receipt."

The sergeant glanced quickly at the constable. Was it possible they had actually caught Rolly out? "No receipt ay?" he said thoughtfully. "That's a bit strange isn't it - not getting a receipt for a valuable bull like that? If you don't mind me askin', Rolly, how much did you pay for him?"

Rolly's groan this time was wrenched from the very depths of his despair. "Twenty bucks," he mumbled.

"Excuse me," the sergeant said as he leaned a little closer. "How much was that?"

As if to reinforce the ludicrous nature of such a meagre price the bull began another bout of furious battering at the insides of the box trailer.

"Twenty bucks, bugger it," Rolly grunted. "An' I'm goin' to lose that an' all if I don't git goin' pretty damn quick."

The two policemen were openly smirking to each other. It seemed they had indeed caught the old rogue out. "You won't mind if I ring through to Colonel Foote for verification then, Rolly?" Although it was politely enough put, the words seemed to imply more threat than question.

"Yer can do what you like," Rolly told him sullenly, "as long as yer do it quick. All I want to do is to git goin' so I can catch the abattoirs before they close."

The sergeant retired to the local police station and rang through to Colonel Foote who verified he had sold a bull to Rolly that morning but, naturally enough, the condition of the bull he described differed markedly with the one Rolly had in his box trailer.

The sergeant hung up the phone thoughtfully. Outside the sounds of the bull thrashing about inside the box had not diminished. He was sure Rolly was trying to pull a swifty but at the moment had no idea what that might be. Perhaps Rolly had switched animals? He decided eventually it was fair enough to take both Rolly and bull back for a proper identification...

An hour or so later the Colonel did confirm it was the same bull he had sold to Rolly that morning for twenty dollars, but at the same time he went to great lengths to point out to the sergeant what its condition was when he had sold him. "He was nigh on dead this morning ... I just can't believe..." The Colonel's voice choked a little as he withdrew his handkerchief from his top pocket and hurriedly coughed into it.

The sergeant was surprised by the Colonel's emotional response. It wasn't like him at all. He was also surprised by Rolly's innocence. In fact you could say he was well and truly pissed-off; after all his good work he had lost his prime suspect once again.

Rolly was also a mite pissed-off because he had missed out on getting the animal to the abattoir that day and wasn't at all sure whether there would be anything left of his horse-box come the next morning if he left him in there. Neither did he have any safe place to keep him over night on his small dilapidated farm. It was a bad day all round.

But Rolly being the operator he was, wasn't going to quit that easily. He decided it was time for a bit of old-fashioned country bargaining. "Look here, Colonel," he said, staring hard at the sergeant, "I've had quite a bit of unnecessary trouble with that bull of yours today. He's cost me one way or another, an' as yer can see he ain't quite as sick as yer thought he was. So how about yer pay me what I've lost an' take the bugger back?"

The Colonel thought about it for a while. The bull's health had certainly taken a turn for the better, and even if he did go into another decline the Colonel was pretty sure he'd still be able to get his hundred dollars or so for old Caesar later as dog meat - which was the original intention anyway. He suspected the bull's sudden turn-about had more to do with Russ Chalmers' injections than anything Rolly might have doctored him with.

"How much?" he asked cautiously. "Seventy bucks," Rolly replied. "The twenty I paid for him and fifty more for me trouble."

"Make that a round fifty and it's a deal," the Colonel told him.

"Done," Rolly said, and before anyone could reconsider he had backed the trailer into the Colonel's bull paddock and released the bolts at the rear end. The bull, feeling something finally give way, lurched backwards and found himself back in his old home paddock. He shook his head a few times as if to clear it of the day's muddle and then decided to take it out on someone. The two policemen were nearest so he put his head down and charged.

The sergeant went up a nearby Kentish cherry tree and the constable just beat the bull to the nearest fence. Next it was Rolly's box trailer that suffered the onslaught of the bull's spite. Two great thumps and one side caved in. Rolly and the Colonel leapt for the ute and took off across the small paddock to the gate with the bull in hot bellowing pursuit.

At the front door of his house the Colonel handed Rolly a cheque for fifty dollars. He resented handing over another thirty dollars for his own bull but at least had the satisfaction of knowing that the latter contract had been couched in terms of expenses rather than income. And, by God, that would be the way he would tell the sorry story to anyone who was pokey enough to ask.

Like the bull before him, Rolly also thought he deserved some kind of retribution for his aggravation. He waved the cheque under the policemen's eyes. "I trust you two blokes are reliable witnesses enough to speak up for me in case I get picked up by one of your lot when I cash this at Conolly's pub this evenin'?"

And just to ram home his advantage he added a couple of lines from his own special brand of homespun country philosophy to the police sergeant before him. "D'y'know what the trouble with this world is, Sarge?" he said. "There just ain't no trust any more, that's what."

Under the circumstances there wasn't much the cops could say - or do. Other, that was, than to vow there and then that they would get Rolly sometime, somehow, if it was the last thing they ever did.

The Amazing Resurrection of Grandma Pike

In her middle seventies Grandma Pike was known in the district of Montvale as a tough old bird. In spite of a touch of arthritis in her hands, brought on by more years of milking cows than she cared to remember, she still persisted in going about her work without complaint. It was, therefore, a surprise to everyone when the word got around that she had suddenly fallen gravely ill and wasn't expected to recover.

When her many relatives heard the news they came from far and wide to pay their last respects to a grand old lady. One of her relatives was a grandniece called Sharon who had made her name in the city as a beautician. Sharon knew all about moisturisers and powders and rouge and lipstick and false eyelashes - what to do about unwanted facial hair and liver-spots and skin webbing caused by too many years of exposure to life's natural elements. It was said that Sharon Pike was a bit of a genius when it came to pitting her skills against the ravages of time.

Certainly old Mrs Pike knew it. "Is that Sharon coming," she demanded all morning through the bedroom door, opened a crack, but not too much. She wanted privacy in her last hours, she told her husband, but not to be cut off entirely from the living just yet. "Certainly not until Sharon comes." She was very insistent about it. "I want to see Sharon before I see anyone else. I want to see the gel the moment she arrives."

It was all a bit puzzling to her husband, seeing Mrs Pike had never particularly showed much interest in Sharon before. "A bit up herself" was more his wife's summation of their city grandniece. And it was all very annoying to the other relatives, especially the two daughters-in-law who surmised the old lady's sons should take precedence over a distant grandniece. Did it mean that Sharon, being the favoured one, was likely to get the pick of the old lady's goodies? That lovely little mother-of-pearl hair brush and mirror, that gipsy table and chair, the fine lacework that old Mrs Pike had sacrificed her eyes for ... those much admired delicate intricate designs that graced every table and sideboard in the old house.

And what of those two genuine Persian rugs that had come down through the family? Too precious to walk on, they hung now at each end of the living room. Then there was that beautiful antique Spode tea-set that Grandpa Pike had given her as a special celebration for the birth of their second son Ray. Who hadn't marvelled at the eggshell lightness of the hand-painted china teacups and saucers? Surely, by all rights, Ray should get that. Yet there was Grandma Pike constantly calling for a grandniece who rarely visited the old lady anyway. Why Sharon in particular? Weren't they all a bit special to the old lady? The mystery of it all kept them all on the edges of their seats in the living room, wondering.

Sharon finally arrived - carefully stepping out of her trim little red car and up the gravel path, jauntily swinging her little purple bag of cosmetic tricks that her great aunt had insisted she bring with her, looking for all the world like she'd just stepped out of a fashion magazine. And undoubtedly there was a collective drawing in of breaths at the sight of her from all those older male relatives who had spilled out on to the verandah for a breath of air and a fag. Cor, what a stunner! They'd almost forgotten. And every one of them must have given a bit of an inward sigh for one thing or another that was lost in the past.

Then there were the younger fry, the gangling cousins - the gawky ones who hid their excitement behind their ruddy-faced smiles of welcome, all the while sneaking furtive looks at Sharon's long shapely legs dancing up the steps towards them. Then each one, old and young alike, in turn giving it away by drawing heavily at their hand-rolled fags as her tantalising perfume wafted under their noses when she passed. Phew!

The rest, the women of the family mostly, said hello to Sharon politely enough for her mother's sake, but their smiles too were as false as Sharon's healthy colour and fluttering eyelashes. Their thoughts were more controlled than their male counterparts but no less envious. Now just look at her! That girl had always had it too easy! Squeezing everything she wanted out of her unfortunate parents - which included two expensive years at an exclusive girl's school in the city from which she vaulted her way into the social scene and eventually into the arms of a well-heeled husband. Well you tell me! And now it looked as though she was going to have first pick again.

But their envy and resentment was mostly for nothing really, for when Sharon finally lowered herself on to her Aunt's bedside chair she, at least, realised immediately the old lady was wanting rather than giving. "Sharon, dear," the old lady whispered, "I want you to do the job of a lifetime on me ... that's why I sent the message to bring your tools of trade. I want you to create the miracle of your professi'n. I want you to make me as radiantly beautiful as I looked when I was a bride. Will you do that for your poor old auntie?"

In fact old Mrs Pike had never been the radiantly beautiful type, her attributes were more of the functional kind. She had been a fine strong girl in her youth, with a complexion more ruddy than radiant and a body more suited to digging spuds and wrestling recalcitrant poddies into their drinking bays than knocking the boys over when she was tripping the light fantastic in the local dance hall.

Nevertheless, Sharon took the request with some seriousness. She cast a speculative gaze at her great aunt's time-ruined face and knew it wasn't going to be any easy road, but yes, try she certainly would. After all her reputation was at stake, and to Sharon that was far more important than any dinner set or mouldy old rug, neither of which would suit her suburban brick mansion in the exclusive end of town anyway. Sharon decided that if her great aunt's final wish was for a miracle, then a miracle it would be.

It took all the morning and half the afternoon to eventually satisfy her great aunt. The old lady looked at her changing complexion a hundred times over in the pearl-shell mirror, turning her head this way and that with surprising agility for someone who was supposed to be hearing the celestial bells calling. Bobbing about like a turkey in a tree, Sharon thought but didn't, of course, say. Patiently she continued, smiling encouragingly all the while, dabbing and smoothing the offending spots, a little more rouge here, a little less powder there. And although at times she found the going tedious she also found inspiration in her great aunt's dedication and single-mindedness, for the old lady uttered not a word of complaint about any of the scraping and snipping. Most of her customers in the city groaned and squealed when the hair roots were merely stunned by the hot tickle of electrolysis. Her great aunt on the other hand, in spite of her weakened state of health, insisted on a tweezers job and bore the pain of uprooting with a fortitude and stoicism even someone as self-centred as Sharon could not help but admire.

It wasn't until mid-afternoon that the old lady was finally satisfied with Sharon's efforts, and it was only then she consented to see the remainder of her relatives. She gazed into the mirror for the hundredth time, flexing, grimacing, and finally smiling. "Gawd, Sharon," she whispered hoarsely, "you're a real little artist, ain't you!"

Sharon gave her a quiet smile, which was as much for her own satisfaction as it was for her aunt's, and went back into the dining room to give the rest of the restlessly waiting relatives the green light.

One by one they trooped into the old lady's room, some bravely hiding their tears and others openly weeping. Old Mrs Pike lay back in her pink pillows with apricot-coloured lace edging, wearing a wan and fatalistic smile on her heavily made-up face which, if not as youthful looking as the old lady thought, certainly retained an air of country regality. "Don't be sad," she told each one of them. "I'd rather go now while I still have my good looks than when I'm old and ugly!" She smiled, feebly and bravely, as she grasped each hand and puckered her ruby lips for the final kiss. "I've had a good life ... I'm happy with my family around me ... that's all that counts."

"Poor old thing ... what a wonderful old lady," a second cousin remarked tearfully when she emerged from the bedroom. A sentiment that, judging by the concerted nose-blowing and fluttering of handkerchiefs, all agreed with.

Finally it was Grandpa Pike's turn to pay his final respects. He made his way sadly into her room. He sat in the bedside chair and took hold of his wife's hand. In Grandpa Pike's eyes his partner of forty-five years was indeed beautiful. As beautiful as the day they got married. Tears streamed down his cheeks as he sat there gazing soulfully into her eyes. Grandma Pike squeezed his hand and told him what she had told all the others; only with Grandpa Pike she added just one regret about her life, and that was his possible infidelity all those years ago with the red-haired dairy maid who came to work for them briefly when Grandma Pike had gone off to hospital to give birth to their second son.

"It has always troubled me, dear heart," the old lady confessed. "Not so much that you may have been unfaithful ... I could have lived with that. After all, dearest, you'd been very restrained while I was carrying Ray. No, dearest, it's the not knowing that makes me so sad. I think I could go to my grave quite happy, even if it was true, but I couldn't do that if I thought you had lied to me."

Grandpa Pike was so moved by his partner's plea he broke down into unrestrained grief. His whole body shook with his sobbing, and his tears which had been trickling down his cheeks, now ran like a flood. His wife offered him a weak smile and gave his hand another squeeze, only this time Grandpa Pike thought he detected a slight fading of her strength. He looked anxiously into his wife's face and saw her purply-tinged eyelids begin to flutter. Little trickles of powder were loosening from her trembling cheeks. She was trying to speak.

He leaned forward to hear the words that came with small puffs of breath into his ear. "Please ... tell me the truth, dearest ... for the sake of your soul ... as well as mine."

Grandpa Pike could control himself no longer. All those years he had managed to keep his guilty secret safe. But now, in these special circumstances...? It just didn't seem right to deny his lifetime mate the truth. "Yes," he confessed suddenly, "it is true ... but only once ... and I didn't really like it at all."

As he gazed into Grandma Pike's eyes with the relieved, wet-eyed expression of a man who had finally made his restitution he was surprised to see, rather than the peace she had promised, a very definite look of triumph. He was even more surprised when he saw her suddenly throw back the covers and begin struggling out of bed and into her slippers. "You skinny little blackguard," she shouted wrathfully. "I knew it! It was that flamin' tea-set that give you away!"

She grabbed up the old dogwood walking stick that she kept by her bed and grasping it tightly in her gnarled old hand she took a vicious swing at her startled mate. There was nothing left for Grandpa Pike to do but run towards the bedroom door, which he did with some alacrity. But Grandma Pike wasn't satisfied with just one swipe at her mate. She was after his blood. Still swinging the walking stick around her head like she was warding off a plague of locusts she staggered after him.

Relatives scattered in all directions as Grandpa Pike charged into the living room at such speed he collapsed right across the afternoon tea table sending plates of scones and cakes in all directions. Hot on his tail Grandma Pike managed to get one good thwack across his buttocks with the walking stick before he recovered his balance enough to scramble his way across the wrecked table to the french windows that led to the verandah.

But neither, it seemed, was one good strike going to satisfy Grandma's Pike lust for revenge. Without hesitation, and with an agility that belied both her years and her poor state of health, she scrambled after

...Grandma Pike wasn't satisfied with just one swipe ...

her fleeing mate, thwacking furiously and threateningly at the air between them.

Thus the pursuer and the pursued lumbered their way down the garden path until they eventually disappeared from sight into the high grass and scrub that grew alongside the creek. The sounds of the chase and the periodic thwacks and cries of Grandpa Pike floated up to the startled relatives who clustered around the open french windows trying to get a better look at the amazing resurrection of Grandma Pike.

Eventually it was up to Sharon - who through her unwitting efforts had made the whole eccentric charade possible and who one way or another in the process had stamped her future claim as the emerging matriarch of the Pike clan - to organise the remainder of the day.

"Well," she said brightly, "it seems as though the old dear has taken a turn for the better, God bless her. Perhaps we should clear up this mess and all go home? There doesn't seem much else we can do at this point, wouldn't you all agree?"

Except for the three great-grandchildren, who had entered into the spirit of the proceedings by conducting their own game of chasing round the piles of broken plates and scattered cakes, no-one else had any objections to such an eminently sensible suggestion.

Though whether it was Grandpa Pike's final confession that gave new life to Grandma Pike, or whether she had set the whole thing up in the first place was never really revealed. All that everyone close to her did know for sure was that Grandma Pike's amazing resurrection lasted for another nine years. She survived her wayward husband by only a few months. And it was always said that other than when she was asleep, she rarely, if ever, in those nine years allowed Grandpa Pike out of her sight.

The Year of the Cherry

Most of the old hands in the district could remember 1937. It was, they said, a bugger of a year for money but a great year for cherries and it was the cherries rather than the hard times that stuck in their minds.

Jimmy Spratt the bootmaker explained. "Them cherries got to be a kind of legend that year, as did the events that followed twenty-one years later." Jimmy gave a bit of a smile then. It was obviously a story he liked to tell. "Though to be even more accurate, it wasn't so much the cherries themselves as it was the cherry wine that followed. I was only a youngster at the time but if my memory serves me correct it was rather unusual weather that year. First a warm dry spring followed by a real wet Christmas and the hottest summer on record."

According to Jimmy, the Parkers owned a small property next door to Cec Jones. "There was a small cherry orchard at the back of the dairy, though one you wouldn't normally take much notice of. A bit scraggly, you know. A bit discarded like. Even by us kids. Cherries not at all like the big fat ones you get these days. Sour as hell and all pip, them cherries were. Though the leaves in the autumn were real pretty as I remember.

"Anyway, that year it was different. In the hot wet summer the cherries grew rounder and redder than you ever seen. The boughs were dragged down with the weight. Even the starkies gave up on them in the end and went after the corbie grubs instead. Parker and his missus picked an' bottled as many as they could between milkings. In the hard times they had some sort of an idea they'd sell 'em later either as jam or preserves. Y'know to supplement the small income they got from the produce of their few dairy cows.

"An' I reckon you could say them cherries got to be some kind of obsession with the Parkers. If they weren't milkin' they was pickin' cherries, an' if they weren't pickin' cherries they was stewin' 'em on their old wood stove and spoonin' them inter Fowler jars. It seemed like they was determined not ter waste one single cherry. Gawd only knows when they found the time to sleep."

Jimmy also remembered that Mrs Parker was eight months pregnant at the time and had later blamed that cherry harvest for the premature birth of her only child Kevin. A peculiar kid from all accounts, according to Jimmy Spratt. He reckoned young Kevin spent more time with the farm animals than he did with his parents when he was growing up. If visitors arrived at the Parkers' place it wasn't an uncommon sight to see young Kev divin' under the house alongside half a dozen barn cats and a dog or two. The Parkers would have to coax him out with cakes and lollies so as they could show him off to their friends.

"Not," Jimmy added, "that he was much to show off, mind. To tell yer the truth he was a bit of a runt all around. I dunno for sure but I reckon Kev's peculiar manner was more due to the fact Mrs Parker was somewhat too old to be havin' kids. Anyway, when Kev did arrive so suddenly, it looked like them cherries had won the day. On his own Parker didn't have a tick's chance in a sheep dip of keepin' up with them. As fast as he picked them, the more got ripe."

According to Jimmy's memory of the events it would have all stopped right there if it hadn't been for someone suggesting to the Parkers that cherries made good wine. Why not, Parker had thought. If bottled cherries commanded some sort of price on the open market, why not cherry wine? Besides, just shaking the fruit off the trees and straining the rubbish out later seemed a whole lot faster and less trouble than bottling and jam making.

The story goes that during the next few days Parker went around the district scrounging every barrel or container he thought might be suitable for maturing wine in. He also spent many hours reading - studying up on the art of wine-making, because he was the sort of bloke who always wanted to do it right. And apparently his dedication paid off. Parker, it seemed, turned out to be something of a natural wine-maker. He eventually managed to mature over a hundred gallons of the stuff and in spite of the hard times - or perhaps because of them - he had no trouble unloading most of it. All business contracted on the quiet out of the back door of his dairy of course - he didn't want the local pub keeper to hear about it and dob him in for being the counterpart of a Tennessee moonshiner.

"Though mind you," Jimmy Spratt said, "the brew Parker had concocted was no less potent than any corn liquor a moonshiner could come up with an' its one an' only public airin' proved that. A saw-miller from up on the Tiers had heard about Parker's wine-makin' activities an' decided a few gallons of cherry wine seemed like a more interestin' proposition than the usual barrel of beer to celebrate the weddin' of his youngest daughter Valerie. He and his missus made up a very decorative punch from it. A bit of this an' a bit of that - even a few petals floatin' on th' top - but solidly underpinned with ten gallons of cherry wine. It sat in th' middle of the table in th' community hall - a cream can full of it. Th' weddin' guests, especially the ladies, took to it like kids to cordial, it tasted so nice. Not surprisingly after an hour or two most of th' weddin' guests were pretty much under the weather, too much so I reckon, an' that's when the trouble started. There was some bad blood between some of the bride's family an' the groom, yer see. Talk of shotgun weddin's an' the like.

"Under the influence of Parker's wine, it was insults that was first thrown, then buttered scones, then cream cakes an' jellies. Even the ladies got stuck inter it. When the bride got a bowl of trifle over her head it was on for young an' old. An all-in brawl like never before's been seen in this district. It could have been the shortest marriage ever if the local cop hadn't arrived ter cool things down a bit. An' th' followin' day it wasn't much better. Th' cheese factory was hours behind schedule, no bread got baked, no groceries delivered. The co-op store didn't even bother to open, an' I seem to remember everyone was creepin' about in a very dismal manner. So yer can see how it was that Parkers wine got ter be so famous, ay?"

According to Jimmy, Parker had apparently decided it best to withdraw his wine from the market after that little fiasco. There was talk in the town of the marriage annulment and of court cases pending, and sooner or later Parker knew the local cop was goin' to come knocking on his door, lookin' for the real source of th' row. The story goes Parker panicked and poured most of what was left into the dairy drain.

"All except one eighteen gallon wooden barrel, that was," Jimmy said. "There was a bit of th' artist in Parker. He couldn't bear ter see all his recent creation bein' used as drain cleaner so he'd hidden that keg under his house, an' if it was found he was goin' ter pledge it was for future personal use, Kev's twenty first in fact.

"A crazy story no doubt," Jimmy said, "but I'll swear that's the way it went. An' that's th' way Parker always told it. He made the excuse in his own mind it was a matter of his wine needin' a bit of maturin' to calm it down before it was ready for another public release. An' I guess y'could say that over the years the anticipation grew. It had a definite use-by date yer see an' Kev's twenty-first was it - another hell of a party.

Jimmy Spratt gave another of his chuckles. "The result of all that was people was forever lookin' to young Kev. Y'know, wonderin' how old he was, an' how many more years it might be ter his twenty-first. An' naturally enough, as the time did come closer, so the legend grew. What would a barrel of twenty-one year old cherry wine be like, ay? The first release had tasted well enough, but what about now it was soaked in wood for so long? Whatever, there was not one solitary soul who knew about the wine that didn't think it would be anything less than potent - lethal even."

Jimmy Spratt stopped to roll one of his cigarettes. There was a kind of half-joking, serious wondering in his expression as he rolled the tobacco back and forth in his hand. He winked as he licked the paper together and popped it in his mouth. Jimmy was telling his story and telling it his way.

"As it turned out there was only one that got to find out. Yer see, it went like this. In the middle of January 1958 the time arrived. Kev's twenty-first. A barrel tappin' ceremony was set for five o'clock in the afternoon, the exact time Kev was born. The first ceremony was set for th' Parkers' relatives an' friends but later there was goin' ter be a more public affair with a harvest dance in Cec Jones' unused apple shed next door. Old man Parker had quipped he felt his wine needed a preliminary run after so long, an' that if the Parker clan were still alive an' kickin' come dance time it would be on fer young an' old."

Jimmy described how the friends and relatives of the Parkers that afternoon had trundled behind old man Parker, cups an' mugs at the ready, to the dugout space under the house. A heavy barn-type door, locked all those years against thievery with a heavy padlock that only Parker had a key to, hidden deep in the back of the kitchen cutlery draw. Dark inside, only one light bulb dangling from the low ceiling, cobwebs everywhere, and then the mighty barrel itself sitting on its runners in the far corner, waiting; looking more like it was a hundred years old rather than just twenty-one.

"Well," said Jimmy, "we all watched breathless as old man Parker cleaned off the barrel with an old broom, tapped out the wooden bung with his hammer and inserted the tap in one easy motion without leakage. Done very neat for a man who'd only read how in a book. But then all was not quite as it seemed yer see - because when Parker turned on th' tap nothin' at all came out. There was no steady flow of the famous twenty-one year old wine like it should've. There wasn't even a flamin' dribble. Very embarrassing for old Parker, I might add. He wrenched at that tap so vigorous like, it eventually came away altogether an' still nothin' came out. Someone at the back suggested rather lamely that it might have gone solid after so many years, an' that remark only helped inflame Parker's agitation. He gave the barrel a whack with his hammer and it sounded anythin' but solid. Hollow as a drum was more like it.

"Well, I tell you, that's when old Parker did his narna real proper. He lets out this mighty grunt an' lifts that barrel clear over his head, then he brings it down with such a hell of a thump that the darn thing splits open from one end to th' other, revealin', I might add, a very pink, very empty inside. Everybody crowded in then to get a good look. An', would yer believe, there was this second bung hole on the top back of th' barrel. A good deal smaller mind you. Jus' big enough ter fit a thin hose inter if needed. Well, it didn't take old Parker long to work that one out. 'Bloody hell,' he shouted, 'Kevin! No wonder we could never find the little bugger! No wonder he's always been a bit dopey. An' where is he now? When I catch him, I'm goin' to flamin' well kill 'im!'

It was then everybody present realised they hadn't see Kevin at all that day. The birthday boy was nowhere in sight. It was a mystery to everyone and it wasn't until the following day word got around he was hiding out at his auntie's place. He sent word back via one of his cousins that he intended to stay there until his old man had signed on a stack of Bibles in front of several witnesses he wouldn't carry his threat of murder out."

Jimmy Spratt said he had never worked out whether it was the eighteen gallons of cherry wine Kev had been into for most of twenty-one years that accounted for his insatiable liking for grog, or whether he'd been driven to drink later by his old man's constant grizzling about his lost wine.

"Whatever reason," Jimmy said, "I've never seen a man before or since who could put it away like Kev Parker could. When his parents died he couldn't sell that little farm up quick enough an' clear out to the city. I reckon it was too risky for a man like Kev to go on livin' in a town with only one pub."

Willum and the Tax Men

Rolly Hills dropped in to Nola Prate's farm one afternoon about afternoon tea time and over a cup of tea he suggested that old Willum Haas might be going round the bend.

"I was up at his place this mornin'," he explained. "He had ten of his best yearling heifers shut up in his loadin' yard an' when I asked him if he was goin' to sell 'em he told me he wasn't. He told me - would you believe - that the reason they was in the yard was because he was teachin' them a lesson."

Nola Prate smiled a bit. "So what, Rolly? That don't make him crazy."

Rolly wasn't convinced. "Don't it now? Then what if I told you they was there because they kept breakin' out of their paddock, an' in old Willum's words, he'd given 'em a fair trial, found 'em guilty, an' sent them to gaol for a few days?"

Nola didn't seemed impressed or surprised. Old Willum had been baling her hay for the past twenty years and she had witnessed many such eccentricities. "If old Willum's got his heifers shut up you can be sure there's a good reason for it, Rolly," she said. "Though the reason might be a little hard to fathom for most. Perhaps his heifers were locked up in his yard to give him the time to fix his fence. That don't make him crazy does it? I reckon he's just having you on, an' you just won't see it because you are still smartin' over the time he did you over."

The incident Nola was referring to was the time when Rolly had bought six jersey heifers from old Willum that might or might not have been in calf. Rolly had cast a lightening quick eye over the heifers which were so huge-gutted they literally waddled into the loading yard. It was

Rolly's estimation they were all very likely heavily in calf and the price Willum was asking seemed very reasonable.

Unfortunately for Rolly, by the time he had trucked them down to the coast where he knew there was a farmer willing to pay premium prices for in-calf heifers, their respective guts had subsided rather dramatically. It was a very forlorn bunch of bony-hipped poddies that he unloaded into the farmer's yard, and a very dirty truck they left behind. The floors and sides of the truck ran with the smelliest, runniest manure you'd be likely to see this side of the abattoir.

Enough of it, the farmer had suggested, to fertilise a four acre spud paddock. If, that was, it didn't look so bloody poisonous!

Rolly, naturally enough, wasn't very amused and the upshot was he had to accept a price much less than he'd expected. He worked out that, what with the hire of the truck and the petrol, he wasn't going to make a cracker out of the deal. And that wasn't to mention he was duty bound to return the truck in the same pristine condition he got it.

To put it bluntly Rolly was pretty pissed-off that day, and even more so later when he found out Willum had been running the heifers on strawberry clover all the week and they were in-gas rather than in-calf. The trip down to the coast had simply shaken the gas out of them, one way or another. It was something a smart operator like Rolly didn't like being reminded of.

"Yeah well," he said to Nola, "I still ain't convinced. I reckon the real reason those pods nearly blew up was more to do with stupidity than cunnin'. I'll bet you the old bastard din' even know what he was doin'. I reckon he was dead surprised I gave him his price without arguin'."

Nola smiled. "Well I reckon you're wrong, Rolly. I reckon he set you up. I mean," she said, boring it in even further, "who better to take down than a smart operator like yourself, ay? And if you want further proof that he's as shrewd as a wall-eyed crow, then what about the time he done over them two city taxmen."

Rolly sipped at his tea a little resentfully. He hadn't dropped in on Nola just to hear how smart old Willum was when he knew damn well that he was as crazy as a headless chook. But, nevertheless, any info he could get on how to win out over the tax department could be valuable.

"Okay, Nola," he said finally, "prove me wrong."

"Well," she said, "it was a couple of years back when those two taxmen turned up at Willum's farm an' wanted to see his books. Well, you know old Willum's barterin' system, Rolly, he never buys or sells anythin' for money, certainly not by bank cheque. Like the truck load of spuds he changed me for my three heifers, an' which later he swapped for Albie Jones' stump-jump plough. Then there was another time he swapped me one of his heifers for a litter of weaner pigs. Nobody ever saw the flash of money in any of them transactions did they? The fact is old Willum never does anythin' ordinary."

... before they left they warned old Willum they'd send him a letter when they got his receipts deciphered.

Nola filled up Rolly's cup again and pushed the plate of scones closer to him. "Anyway," she continued, "by the time old Willum had dragged out six sugar bags of rough scribbled notes an' receipts, dating back, I might add, to the horse and buggy era, them taxmen must have known they was in for a long stay. When one of them suggested to Willum with some aggravation that it was all a bit of a mess Willum pleaded lack of schoolin'. So they suggested that maybe Willum could get some help from an accountant, or maybe someone in the district who knew about figures. Old Willum scoffed at that suggestion too. He told them taxmen that there was no-one in the district he could trust and he certainly wasn't goin' to let any stranger go poking into his business."

Nola smiled. "It took them two unfortunate men three whole days to do a stock-take of old Willum's machinery. As you well know Rolly, he's got stuff up there datin' back to the pioneers, an' he stows it in heaps. Them taxmen must have thought they was on an archi-logical expedition, diggin' their way into that lot. It took 'em nearly all of one day just to find his potato plough. I'll tell you Rolly, those taxmen were nearly frantic by the fourth day. It seemed like they was goin' to have to spend the rest of their lives doin' old Willum over."

Nola went on to explain how even old Willum had seemed to take pity on the two eventually. "So you see, Rolly, as some kind of consolation at the end of the week he arranged with Mrs Haas to get the taxmen a nice hot meal. You wouldn't believe - the meal she put on the table consisted of a bowl of over-stewed turnips mixed with what looked like a heap of whole grain barley and a lump of greasy mutton that was so full of maggots it looked like it was in danger of crawling right off the kitchen table and out the nearest door. Those two taxmen took one look at that meal and turned pea-green. They decided then they'd do the rest of old Willum's business back in the city after all. But before they left they warned old Willum they'd send him a letter when they got his receipts and bits and pieces deciphered."

Nola continued. "Well, old Willum was having none of that either Rolly. He reminded them again of his lack of schoolin'. He told them it was no good sending him any letters because he couldn't read or write, an' when the other geezer had suggested they would ring him, old Willum told him his phone line was down and he couldn't afford the wire to fix it. Them two poor men finally left in despair, an' in such a hurry one of them even forgot his coat was still hanging in Willum's back porch. As far as I know he never returned to claim it. I reckon in the end they dropped old Willum's tax demand in the too-hard basket."

Nola Prate gave a quiet chuckle. "Of course, when them two taxmen was gone, Willum took that 'nice hot meal' out an' dumped it back in the pig bin - that's where it had come from in the first place anyway. No Rolly, you can't kid me old Willum is crazy, he's too damn cunnin'."

She stood up then and offered Rolly a sly smile. "Now Rolly," she said, "seein' you're here, an' so nicely warmed by my tea an' scones, how'd you like to come out to the bull yard with me an' offer a woman on her own a bit of advice on casteratin' a bull calf?"

The Biggest Cray in the World

The Pelican Hotel, just twelve kilometres down the coast road from Montvale, had never really been considered as a district pub. Other than to sip a beer or two after a day's fishing on the coast, the locals rarely bothered to do any serious drinking there. It was a dilapidated old place built from weather boards and corrugated iron sheets. Other than a couple of electric fans there was no air conditioning of any kind. In the summer the three bars were often comparable to a Turkish bath and in mid-winter to an ice-box. But the pub's location at the mouth of an excellent fishing river and its access to magnificent beaches, all at a cost most families could afford, ensured there were always plenty of city visitors during the summer season.

Cliff Randall, proprietor and owner, used to capitalise on these advantages in two ways. The first was to employ an excellent sea-food cook to keep his clientele happy and the second was to make sure of a steady supply of fresh fish. The fact that just about all of the pub's fish supplies came from the river insured their freshness, and the further fact that just about all of those fish were caught by Cliff's two adult sons, insured that they were as cheap as you could get. The manner in which Cliff's two sons caught the fish, though, was a constant bone of contention to the other serious fishermen in the vicinity. The rumour was the Randall boys got most of their catch early in the morning with illegal river nets. But because nobody had ever actually caught them red-handed there seemed very little anyone could do about it.

A policeman was stationed on the coast but he was never around at the crack of dawn. It was said, by those who knew him, that he was more of an afternoon sort of person. He performed best in the afternoons. Speeding tourists were his main victims, or the occasional rowdy visitor who got a bit boisterous during one of Cliff's special cray-bake beach barbecues.

According to some of the local fishermen there was also the rumour that Cliff's boys had several unregistered cray pots set at various points along the coast, but because nobody had actually caught them at that either, there was little they could do about it. Occasionally, at the request of the fishermen, a fisheries officer would turn up and poke about a bit, but he never found out anything - except perhaps to be aware that whenever he did turn up, fish dishes at Cliff's pub were virtually nonexistent.

... Cliff was as shrewd as a gran'daddy cormorant and as slippery as a river eel.

Donny Conolly, the owner of the only other pub in the near vicinity, especially disliked Cliff. Whenever Cliff's name was mentioned Donny was likely to blow a fuse. "That bludger!" he'd say with considerable venom. "He's a bloody disgrace to all decent publicans. It's my hope that one day he'll get caught out and get his just deserts."

But even that vague hope seemed unlikely because there was no doubt that Cliff was as shrewd as a gran'daddy cormorant and as slippery as a river eel. He always managed to keep himself one step in front of the law, no matter what. Those who had known Cliff for any length of time could recount many tales about his flexible attitude towards honesty, especially when it came to making the odd dollar. But one particular tale that was told about Cliff's shrewdness had become almost legendary throughout the district.

It all began when a fisherman caught what was said to be the biggest crayfish anyone had ever seen. Having viewed the cray himself at the nearby wharf Cliff, being the man he was, immediately saw a way to make a few extra dollars for himself. He offered the fisherman a price he couldn't refuse and took the cray back to his hotel. The following day a large notice written in red crayon appeared in a very prominent position on his pub verandah. The notice read:

> THE BIGGEST CRAY IN THE WORLD
> TO BE RAFFLED SAT. NIGHT NEXT -
> WIN ENOUGH CRAY TO LAST
> THE AVERAGE FAMILY A WEEK!

Sure enough, on the following Saturday night, the pub was packed out with both tourists and locals who had come to take a dekko at the monster cray and, if lady luck was with them, to win it. At nine o'clock, the time when he figured suspense was at its height, Cliff gave the signal for one of his sons to take the cray out of the freezer and wheel it in a barrow around the bars. From feelers to tail it covered the whole bottom of the barrow. The crowd literally gasped at its size. No-one was disappointed. It was truly a monster. Even Ossie Nichols, who was never known for giving praise lightly, was suitably impressed. "Strewth, it's got more body than a suckling pig," he said to his wife.

"Nearly twelve pounds, an' he'll stretch two foot eight," Cliff told everyone proudly. He held up a couple of books of tickets. "Now folks," he shouted, "down to business - who wants to own him?"

There was no shortage of takers and even at the relatively high price of a dollar a ticket Cliff went through the two books in less than fifteen minutes. The local cop, who had just come out of the dining room where he'd been enjoying one of Cliff's complimentary seafood specialities, expressed some doubt about the legality of such a raffle. He didn't want it to get around that he was extending any special favours to Cliff just because Cliff offered him a meal on the house now and again.

"Ar, fair go mate," Cliff said. "What's the harm? After expenses, all proceeds will go to the poor little crippled kiddies, an' they need all the help they can get, don't they."

To convince the cop that the ends did justify the means, Cliff pulled off a few tickets and pressed them into his hand. And later, just to continue to keep things honest and above board, Cliff chose a complete stranger, a respectable-looking blue-rinsed old lady, to draw the winning ticket from her own beach hat.

A tourist, dressed in blue shorts, floral shirt and thongs, waved the lucky winning ticket above his head and his sunburnt face glowed even more redly than the crayfish as he stepped forward excitedly to claim his prize. Cliff shook the tourist's hand warmly and then led him off to the kitchen to arrange transfer of the monster cray.

Meanwhile, in the ladies' lounge and the two bars, all those who didn't win compensated themselves with more drinks and gradually came round to the conclusion that even if they had missed out on a lifetime's chance of getting their hands on the biggest cray in the world it was, after all, in a good cause...

It was, therefore, quite a surprise to all when only a few days after Cliff's successful raffle there appeared a second notice on Cliff's pub verandah declaring a second monster raffle. This time the notice read:

    THE BIGGEST CRAY IN THE WORLD
    TO BE RAFFLED HERE SAT. NIGHT
    (* THE SECOND BIGGEST WAS WON LAST WEEK)

The following Saturday night Cliff's hotel was again packed to the verandahs. If there was a cray bigger than the one that had been raffled the previous week then everyone, it seemed, wanted to clap their eyes on it. Especially, of course, the locals. They were all well aware of Cliff's dubious reputation and were, to say the least, dead curious to find out how Cliff could come up with two freak crayfish in such a short time.

Nevertheless, as it turned out, nobody was disappointed with Cliff's second offering. Perhaps it was bigger than the previous week's offering, perhaps it wasn't. Whatever, it certainly was another monster and all those present were very pleased to get another chance to have a go at picking the winning ticket.

Unfortunately for the locals it was another of Cliff's in-house guests who won the cray and she too went off to the kitchen with Cliff to arrange the transfer of the giant cray, leaving the many losers to wash down their disappointment with a few more beers and console themselves, as they had the week previous, with the now time-worn phrase that win or lose, it was, after all, for a good cause.

By the end of the night when the revellers had finally dispersed to their various accommodations it seemed like it was all over. But once again this wasn't to be the case because, by some sleight of hand that could have only been matched by Houdini, on the following Friday Cliff revealed that he had a third monster cray to be raffled.

By now, the locals, especially the fishermen who hadn't had a particularly good year with their own pots, were beside themselves to find out the source of those crays. What amazing hole could possibly harbour such a heap of gigantic crustaceans? A group of them even got together the following day to try to organise some sort of surveillance on Cliff and his sons; but all to no avail. If the crays were being poached illegally it wasn't being done in any ordinary way. In fact, the information was that Cliff himself rarely left the pub. Neither was any transaction with any person who looked like a possible supplier ever noted. Yet over the following summer period Cliff managed to get his hands on three more of those crayfish that, give or take a pound or two, were of equal startling proportions to the original "world's biggest cray".

The effects of his success with those raffle nights reached far and wide. Certainly it was a strong talking point in the district. Especially with Cliff's rival Donny Conolly who noted a distinct dropping off of his bar trade during that period. It seemed as if many of his regulars had become obsessed with trying to figure out just what Cliff was up to and were willing to travel the extra distance to the coast in the hope of doing so. Besides, there was always the outside chance they could get lucky and win one of those much prized crays themselves.

But, as they say, all good things do come to an end and end it did. A further notice appeared on Cliff's pub verandah several weeks later that stated very succinctly there would be no more cray raffles. When questioned about it Cliff remained tight-lipped. In fact, in contrast to his jovial manner throughout the summer period, he was now downright rude and unapproachable. One would have thought all his beer stocks had suddenly gone flat, or that Russ Chalmers the Health Inspector had threatened him with closure.

It seemed as if the mystery of those crayfish was never going to be solved. Until, that was, Cliff and his seafood cook fell out and she quit her job. The lady got a bit tiddly one night in Connolly's pub and confided the true story to Phylis Barnes, the baker's wife, who spread it around the whole town by ten o'clock the following morning.

It turned out that the crayfish Cliff had been raffling all summer was, in fact, the very same one every time. A freak monster that might only be expected to turn up once in a lifetime. Cliff's little ploy had been to take the winners out to the kitchen where he confessed to each one that the cray had "gone off". One good sniff had been enough to convince them that this was the truth.

According to the seafood cook, Cliff would then further confess that he had realised the cray had been bad when his son was wheeling it around earlier that night, but had kept on because he'd had in the back of his mind how it would be the poor little kiddies who would have dipped out if he had called the raffle off. Cliff then told the winner how he was willing to chuck in half a dozen small crayfish to compensate. "Enough," he would say expansively and with as much charm as he could muster, "to last your family a week."

How could any tourist refuse such a generous offer, especially in the face of his previous heart-rending appeal on behalf of "the poor little crippled kiddies"? To a person, each had succumbed to Cliff's guile, taken their bundle of fresh crayfish, and for the sake of propriety kept their mouths closed. Then, after each one had departed, Cliff, the cunning old sod, would rinse the coating of high-smelling anchovy paste off the giant cray and pop it back into the freezer for the following Saturday.

"To cap off the outrage," the cook told Phylis, "I never heard of any of the money goin' to any deserving cause, other than Cliff himself."

"But how did Cliff know a local wouldn't win the prize?" Phylis wanted to know. "A local would surely have woken up to Cliff's little con."

The seafood cook then revealed the true extent of Cliff's craftiness. She told Phylis that Cliff had used two sets of raffle tickets, one lot for the locals and the other for his hotel guests and casual tourists. The locals' ticket butts had gone into Cliff's pockets rather than the hat.

So why had the whole thing collapsed? Natural justice, that was how. During a wild summer storm the wind dropped a tree fair smack across the power lines along the coast road and in the six hours it took to fix it, most of the food in Cliff's pub freezer had spoiled. Including, of course, the giant cray Cliff had been wheeling around his hot smoky old pub for half the summer season.

The Chocolate Pigs

In the early nineteen-sixties young Tom Wright, an English orphan, had come out to Australia under the Little Brother Rural Program, and even though he had worked on various farms in the district since he was sixteen years old it seemed he was never going to get the hang of farming. The best that anyone could say of him was he was a trier.

But as Harold Bushell said at a farmers' meeting one night when explaining his reasons for sacking young Tom, "Tryin' is a more apt description. I stuck him out for nine months an' I reckon I did my bit for Anglo-Australian relations. I spent more time showin' him things for the hundredth time than was worth it. I finished up doin' his work as well as me own. He's not much better inside, either. Me missus won't let him near the washin' up even. Not worth two knobs of goat's poo, she reckons."

Denny Bourke agreed. "He did some fencin' for me once and the posts were so out of line every time I tightened the wires, staples sprayed out of it like it was a machine gun. The only reason that nothin' got through that fence was because the animals thought it too dangerous to go near. An' it's no good askin' any of the shop-keepers in town to give him a job any more because of that little incident he had with Bob Parker a few months back."

The incident that Denny was referring to was the time when Bob Parker at the hardware store had, in a weak moment, offered to employ young Tom part-time. The job only lasted a week. Poor Tom had tripped over his own feet and dropped a box of imported dinnerware right in the middle of the shop. Nobody could have blamed Bob Parker for getting a bit stroppy and sacking the boy on the spot.

The only person in the district who could afford to carry young Tom with all his inadequacies was Colonel Foote and he wouldn't have a bar of the boy because he reckoned he was inclined to be insubordinate. Which, of course, really meant he was still simmering over the time when, under his own previous employment with the Colonel, young Tom had jacked up on working Sundays without getting paid overtime.

Fortunately for the young lad another chance to reinstate himself in the eyes of the locals came about after Nola Prate was taken ill. The local doc diagnosed Nola's complaint as a hernia and suggested that he should arrange for Nola to go to the city for an operation. Nola complained all over the township about the impossibility of such a thing. Who, she wanted to know, was going to look after her farm and animals while she was languishing in a hospital?

It was Rolly Hills who first suggested young Tom. He had gone to Nola's place to drop off a couple of bags of grain that he had picked up for her at the railway station. "I know young Tom's got a name for bein' a bit hopeless, Nola, but I could keep an eye on him for yer. Any road, at this time of year there's only the house cow to milk, an' the dog an' chooks to be fed. You got a ton of grass yet so I reckon the rest of yer animals can look after themselves."

"And my baconers to be topped off," she reminded him.

On the whole she wasn't at all pleased with the idea. Having Rolly poking around when she wasn't there was bad enough but to have some young whippersnapper mucking things up as well didn't seem much like a reasonable proposition.

"I'll keep an eye on him for yer Nola. I'll look in every mornin' an' every evenin'," Rolly assured her.

Nola wasn't convinced by Rolly's assurances but she really had little choice. If she didn't have her operation before next milking season began she'd have to wait another year and the Doc had insisted that would not be advisable. She finally, albeit reluctantly, agreed to take up Rolly's suggestion and, at the end of the week, packed her bag and went off to hospital with the same degree of anxiety, some said, as a truck load of fat lambs might have felt when they were off loaded at George Saw's slaughter house on the edge of town.

But not before, that was, she had given Rolly and young Tom a long list of written instructions that denied them any possibility of having to make any decisions themselves. Everything was on that list. A day by day, hour by hour description of every detail of work she could think of and every possible contingency that might arise. She even suggested what radio station the old Jersey house cow preferred when being milked. She detailed exactly the amount of grain to feed the pigs and the chooks each day, how long to cook it up in her old dairy copper and how to make sure it was cooled to the exact right temperature before feeding it out.

'With the two bags you brought me last week, Rolly,' she wrote and underlined, 'there's just enough grain in the shed to feed both the baconers and the chooks for the three weeks I'll be away.' She pinned all these instructions on the notice board in her kitchen. There were even some simple recipes for stews and soups on the bottom of the list for young Tom's benefit and a post script instruction on how to work the porta-gas bath heater.

"That list," she insisted to Rolly and young Tom on the morning of her departure, "should be followed to the letter. If you do that, Tom, then nothing can go wrong."

Poor Nola. Being a farmer of many years standing, she should have known better than to tempt fate that way. Not that young Tom didn't follow her instructions explicitly the following day - he did. And just to make sure he was getting it right he raced into the kitchen every few minutes to make certain he'd done exactly as Nola specified. The trouble was, he was so occupied in doing it right he forgot to take heed of those few extra details that Nola hadn't bothered to mention because they were so damn obvious - like making sure that he secured the gate firmly behind him after he fed the pigs.

Consequently, later that morning when he returned to the house yard from checking out the sheep and the cattle in the valley paddocks he was horrified to find Nola's usually pristine house yard a terrible mess. If he hadn't known better he could have thought some kind of whirlwind had struck during his absence. Strewn straw, grain, dust and torn hessian bags lay from one end of the yard to the other. And the six baconers, having gorged their way through their three weeks supply of food in under an hour, were lying in heavenly snoring bliss right smack in the middle of the chaos. Naturally enough, young Tom panicked. He ran from bloated pig to bloated pig, kicking and swearing at them as he tried to drive them back to their pen. By the time he got them all safely locked away he was almost exhausted and close to tears. Once again it seemed his lack of thought and care had demonstrated his gigantic incompetence.

When Rolly arrived later that afternoon and heard the sad story he was appalled. "Strewth young matey," he groaned, "when Nola gets to hear about this she'll more than likely kill us both."

And tears still hovering, all young Tom could do was to nod in miserable agreement.

Rolly, however, was a man of considerable optimism. He tried to cheer up young Tom. "Well, I suppose it could have been worse," he said. "They could have all died from stuffin' themselves with raw grain. What you got to do now is keep yer eye on 'em, an' if they look like they're in pain give me a ring. Meanwhile I'll poke around an' see if I can find a few bags of cheap grain to replace what they ate. They won't need anythin' for a day or two, that's for sure."

But Rolly's optimism was for once misplaced. It had been a bad season for grain and what was available for stock feed was commanding premium prices. He told young Tom the bad news the following morning. Fortunately all the pigs had survived their gluttonous splurge of the previous day and now the immediate problem was to find some alternate food to feed them on for the time Nola was going to be away.

"There must be somethin' we can find." Rolly said. "Has Nola got any turnips in this year? Cabbages? Anythin'?"

Tom shook his head dismally. "The only fing I can fink of is, I let 'em out to graze, Rolly."

Rolly shook his head. "Grazin' will only keep em alive, young matey - it won't fatten 'em. Any road, Nola mightn't approve of her pastures bein' dug up by a heap of hungry pigs. No, we'll just have to keep sniffin' around an' hope somethin' will turn up." Rolly shook his head again in a very uncharacteristic dismal manner. "Though I don't know what, young matey - it's been a rotten week all round."

There was no doubt that both Rolly and young Tom were in big trouble. Nola Prate was not a big woman but she had a reputation in the district of having a pretty ferocious temper. Once she had taken a fern hook to a group of would-be shooters trespassing on her property and it was only their uncommon turn of speed through three paddocks, across a creek and over several fences, that saved them from mortal injury. Nola still had in her possession two of the guns they had dropped in their flight. Better to be deprived of your favourite gun than your life was the local wisdom. The retribution that she might dole out to Tom and Rolly if anything happened to her precious baconers didn't warrant thinking about.

But then fate, no matter how far removed, often takes some strange turns and that very same evening events began to take shape that eventually were to put an entirely new twist to the dilemma. While burning her rubbish in her incinerator at the back of her sweet shop, Amy Pike accidentally set her store shed on fire and in spite of the best efforts of the town's volunteer fire brigade most of her stock was lost to the flames.

It was Rolly who told young Tom about it the following morning. "Poor Amy's in a real tizzy," he said. "Just about all her stock was damaged by the fire, an' what wasn't got ruined by water. Seems like she's havin' the same rotten luck we are."

Young Tom, who was still buried deep in his own troubles, didn't at first respond. He only accepted the news with a brief nod. Until, that was, something deep in his mind clicked into place. His usually rather pasty face suddenly turned red as the idea settled. Then he began a kind of excited twittering. "Mrs Pike's shop you said Rolly din' you? It was Mrs Pike's lovely little sweet shop what got burnt?"

Rolly was sure that the stress of the past couple of days was too much for Tom. He laid his hand on his young friend's shoulder and clucked sympathetically. "Here, take it easy young matey, don't you go blowin' a valve on me now, Nola's pigs ain't all that important."

By this time Tom was shuffling about and clapping his hands excitedly. "I got a great idea Rolly. I reckon we might be able to save the bacon after all. It's real weird but it might jus' work. Why don't we try feedin' those bleedin' pigs on chocs and liquorice all-bleedin'-sorts?"

Rolly looked shocked. "Yer can't feed pigs on lollies, young matey!"

But young Tom wasn't going to be talked out of his brilliant idea so easily. "Why not Rolly? 'ave you ever tried it? I could melt 'em darn an' feed it to 'em like it was 'orlicks or somethin'."

In spite of his lingering doubts Rolly couldn't help getting caught up in young Tom's enthusiasm. Desperate times called for desperate measures. It was a philosophy that had served him well in the past. He shrugged. "Yer might be right young matey, I suppose it wouldn't do no harm to give it a go. I mean, sugar's been known to fatten dogs ain't it."

The upshot was they rang Amy and offered her a small price for her damaged stock. Amy was only too pleased to have someone take the problem off her hands, but she was puzzled. "Whatever do you want it for, Rolly?" she wanted to know.

"If I told you Amy," Rolly said with a grimace into the phone, "you'd never believe it."

For his part young Tom had no doubts whatsoever. He was up at the crack of dawn the following morning getting the old dairy copper alight in preparation for what must have been the strangest load of stock feed ever to arrive at Nola Prate's farm. During the following days he spent most of his time unwrapping hundreds of bars of chocolates and lollies and popping them into half-filled buckets of boiling water from the copper. Into this already exotic mixture he also added any other bits and pieces he had managed to scrounge around the town. The resulting mixture was something to behold, and the smell of it right out of this world.

The first time he poured the mixture into the baconers' feeding troughs they sniffed at it rather suspiciously, but after satisfying themselves it was some kind of food after all, they began to tuck in. Whatever their initial doubts, the taste of it seemed very much to their liking. They cleaned up the first two buckets in seconds and began impatiently grunting for more. Young Tom was well and truly chuffed!

As was Rolly who arrived in time for the evening's feeding. He watched in awe as the six pigs demolished the first bucketful. The impression Rolly got was the pigs considered their present fare even more heavenly than their previous unlimited access to the grain shed. They literally fought each other to get their snouts into the feeding trough first.

"Well, I'll be buggered," Rolly said as he watched the pigs finish off the one bucket and scramble after the next. "They sure seem to go on it okay, young matey." Still in wonder he bent down to sniff at the steaming liquid. "Though by crikey I dunno why. The bloody stuff smells like a cross between George Saw's killin' shed an' the bar-room at Conolly's pub on a Saturday night."

Young Tom grinned a bit. "That's probably the stale beer an' the fish heads."

Rolly looked at Tom with disbelief. "Beer an' fish heads! What beer an' fish heads?"

"Fish heads from the cannery darn th' coast. A mate of mine dropped them in earlier. An' like you said Rolly, the dregs from Conolly's pub. I kidded Pat inter drainin' all the stale beer into buckets under the counter."

Rolly shook his head and clucked his tongue in admiration. "Young matey," he said, "up till now you've been missing your true vocation."

By the time Nola returned, the six baconers were a joy to behold. Still a little shaky from her operation, and having recuperated slower than she should because of her continual worry about young Tom and Rolly looking after her interests, she could hardly believe her eyes. She was, to say the least, ecstatic in her praise. "They're a credit to you lad - both you and Rolly. You must have followed my instructions to the letter, ay?"

Young Tom didn't correct her. How could he? As for the pigs? Well, they went off a few days later to the butcher in the next town and that should have been the end of it. But it wasn't - not entirely. Three weeks later the butcher was on the phone to Nola. "Those baconers Miss Prate," he said with a kind of breathless interest, "whatever did you feed them on? I've had my customers returning for seconds and thirds an' still they can't get enough. They reckon it's the sweetest bacon they ever tasted. Have you got any more?"

Nola Prate told him she hadn't but would keep him in mind for her next batch in the spring. She was very pleased that her pigs had acquired such popularity, but had very little idea why; other, that was, than they had been fed on first class grain and she had always declared that grain-fed pigs were best.

But such enthusiasm from a butcher was unprecedented. It continued to tax her brain for some time after. As did the mystery of the many chocolate and sweet wrappers that she kept coming across in the most unlikely places. That young Tom, she thought, must be a closet chocolate eater. She thought it might be something to do with the fact he had been born and bred in London's East End. Which, incidentally, was a point Rolly hadn't missed when he offered young Tom a job as his offsider. "He may be a flop at farmin'," he told Pat the barman one night, "but as a wheeler-dealer he's a right little natural."

Three Birds with One Stone

It got back to the Montvale district that old Cec Jones had died in an old folks' home in the city. The news was greeted with some sorrow. Old Cec had been liked by everyone who knew him and it was said he could not only spin a better yarn than a professional comedian, he could turn the most disastrous of occasions into the funniest thing you ever heard.

It was one of those rainy late spring days when everyone who owned a piece of ground was willing to take it easy for a couple of hours and let the rain do their work for them. Consequently, the main bar of Conolly's pub was quite crowded for a mid-week afternoon and everyone, it seemed, had at least one yarn they could recall about Cec and his past life in the district.

Pat the barman, for instance, reminded those present of the episode involving Cec during the big floods of the sixties. Old Cec had stalled his truck trying to get it across the floodway at the bottom of his property and then tried to pull it out first with his ute and then with his horses. "The end result was," Pat continued, "the whole bloody lot went the same way as his truck, an' even though Cec broke a rib or two that morning savin' his horses, and nearly drowned himself to boot, when he told us the story later you'd swear to God he'd never had so much fun in his life."

And so the stories and jokes went on all afternoon. The result was, by milking time, everyone was feeling somewhat sentimental about the loss of their old mate. Ossie Nichols especially seemed moved by the whole occasion. He suggested to the others that a contingent from the district should attend old Cec's funeral service in the city and pay their final respects to the old bloke.

"We could share transport," he said, "an' you know - make a day of it. See him off proper."

The twelve or so others in the bar concurred, and in the spirit of both commiseration and celebration they drank to Cec's memory and pledged to drive the hundred and fifty kilometres into the city the following day.

Even Herbie Miles, who never had much time for such frivolities agreed to go. But, true to form, Herbie wasn't going to do it the simple way of sharing cars and tossing in petrol money, he was going to do it his way. He decided there and then that he would kill two birds with one stone and take in a load of porkers for the early morning market.

He told his wife Florrie about his decision when he arrived home to help her and their son Clarie to milk the cows that evening. "I'll wash the old ute down before I leave the sale yards an' nobody'll know the difference."

Florrie looked at him with disbelief. "But what about me, Herbert? What about my condition?"

Unfortunately, in planning his trip to the city Herbie had forgotten to take into account that his wife was due to give birth to their third child any day now and the old ute was the Miles' only means of transport.

Herbie grimaced as he changed into his overalls ready for milking. It was time for a bit of quick thinking. "Well," he said eventually, "why don't you and young Gaye come with me. I mean, if in the odd chance you happened to start when we're in the city then no sweat, I can just drop you into the public hospital. If yer don't - well nothin' lost, is it - yer could just go to the District Cottage Hospital later as we arranged. Clarie can start th' milkin' when the bus brings him home from school."

Needless to say, Florrie wasn't too struck with the idea. She had seen many of Herbie's intricate plans go awry in the past and there seemed no reason to believe this particular one would be any different. But she also knew from experience that her Herbie was a stubborn cuss, once he made up his mind about something it took a whole heap of shifting. She gave Herbie a martyr's sigh and reluctantly agreed to do it his way.

The following morning after an early milking, Herbie, Florrie, and their four year old daughter Gaye - who suffered from poor eyesight and eczema - set off for the city in their old ute, its springs literally groaning under the weight of the seven fat porkers in the back. And, whether it was just one of those nasty coincidences, or the bouncing of the ute that did it, not forty minutes along the road Florrie thought she felt her first contraction. "We'd better turn back, Herbert," she said, holding her hand to her huge stomach. "It could be another false alarm but I don't think so."

"Just be quick, Herbert, or there will be two of us to take to hospital..."

But Herbie didn't agree. "Don't worry, old girl, there's still plenty of time to get there. I mean it's almost as far back as it is forward so it seems just as easy to go on, don't it? An' let's face it, yer've had several false alarms in the last few days. It could be just another one. Just another thirty minutes, old girl, an' we'll be there. I'll just speed up a bit, ay."

But as was usually the case Herbie got it wrong. By the time they got to the main highway Florrie's contractions were coming steadily every ten minutes or so and by that time Herbie wasn't feeling quite so confident. "She'll be right," he kept assuring his wife. "We'll make it in time. Don't you worry, ay."

He tried to say it as airily as possible but even he was beginning to feel the pressure. Rather than the firm assurance he intended, his words seemed more of a vague hope. A hope which very soon turned out to be completely unjustified. They had only driven a few more k's down the road when there was a sudden loud explosion from under the floor of the ute. The old banger had blown a tyre.

"Strewth!" Herbie said as he wrestled the bucking ute to the side of the road. "That's bloody well torn it."

Quicker than he had moved for a long time Herbie was out of the ute and surveying the damage. The retread tyre (which Herbie had bought at a bargain price to save money) had peeled off like the skin of a banana. He hurriedly removed his coat and passed it through the window to his wife who, judging by her contorted expression, was into her next contraction.

Unfortunately for Herbie (and especially for Florrie who seemed in danger of having her next offspring right there in the cabin of the ute) there was further disaster on the way. The spare tyre was as flat as the one it had to replace. And just to make matters worse, as Herbie clambered under the back of the ute to let down the spare wheel, he received a considerable dousing of pig's urine on his shirt and trousers.

Not that it worried Herbie much at the time. He had other problems to consider. He told Florrie the bad news about the tyre. "I'll have to get a lift to the nearest garage, old girl. How's it goin'?"

Florrie gave him another quick martyred look as her contraction subsided and, stoic country woman that she was, she waved him on his way. "Just be quick, Herbert," she told him breathlessly, "or there will be two of us to take to hospital."

In the first bit of good luck for the day Herbie got a lift almost immediately from another farmer also heading for the market. The farmer dropped him off at a garage not far down the road. A little wild-eyed by now, Herbie explained his dilemma to the mechanic who immediately swung into action. He dropped what he was doing and set about fixing Herbie's tyre.

Ten minutes later he drove Herbie back down the road and changed the wheel for him. It cost Herbie the expected profit on two of his porkers but in the circumstances even someone as careful with their money as Herbie wasn't going to quibble over a few dollars. He waved the mechanic a quick farewell and charged on to the hospital.

By the time they got there Florrie was in hard labour and it was a very relieved Herbie who passed his wife into the care of the hospital staff. Because of the tyre mishap Herbie was still in a hurry. A quick look at the clock showed him that the market had already begun.

"I'll be back as soon as Cec's funeral service is over," he shouted after Florrie as the mobile stretcher disappeared through the swing doors of the maternity wing. "An' don't yer worry about Gaye. I'll keep me eye on her."

At the market the stock agent only just managed to get Herbie's pigs into a pen in time for the sale though he wasn't all that hopeful that Herbie would get the price he expected. He told Herbie that porkers had been a reasonable price earlier but because of an oversupply they were beginning to drop.

"Still, Mr Miles," the agent told him. "yours look okay, it might be all right."

As it turned out it was a far too optimistic opinion. Herbie was offered a very poor price and understandably he wasn't too happy. Not only did he have the cost of a new inner tube and tyre repairs to catch up with, he also had his petrol money to take into account. "I could have done better with the local butcher," he complained to the agent.

But no matter how he protested the buyers wouldn't budge. It was inevitable Herbie was going to get stubborn, and get stubborn he did. He told everyone there to stuff their price, he was going to take the porkers back home and if need be he would take them on to baconers. Of course Herbie then had to load his pigs back on board the ute and the extra time involved again made him late for his next appointment - old Cec's funeral service.

By the time he and Gaye arrived at the city crematorium it was past the time the service was due to begin. Herbie hurriedly parked his old ute in the only available space beside a brick wall. By now his load of pigs, which hadn't been fed since the previous night, were beginning to show signs of impatience. There was an increasing tendency for them to squeal in a very bad-tempered manner.

Herbie shut his ears to their clamour and with Gaye in reluctant tow he trotted off along the short path to the crematorium. Through the open door he could see that the place was already packed out. It seemed old Cec's happy disposition had, since his retirement, won him as many friends in the city as it had in the country.

Herbie decided it was best his daughter waited outside during the service. It was a pleasant sunny day so he sat her on a small lawn adjacent to the chapel with the colouring book and pencils that Florrie had the foresight to bring with them. "Funerals aren't very nice for little girls," he told her. "You just stay here and do a bit of colourin' in until daddy comes back."

Even though the child stared sullenly to the front and refused to give the book and coloured pencils the least acknowledgment she didn't protest so, satisfied that she would be safe there, Herbie hurried across to the crematorium chapel and squeezed his way through the doors just before the usher closed them.

He found Ossie Nichols and the others at the back of the packed room and sidled up beside them. Ossie gave him a quick nod. "How'd yer go with yer pigs, Herbie?" he asked in the kind of hushed whisper he thought appropriate to his surroundings.

Herbie merely shrugged. He didn't want to talk about it and chance the possibility that Ossie might gloat over his misfortune.

However, it wasn't the misfortune of not selling his pigs that eventually caught up with Herbie, it was more to do with the puncture he had earlier. The room was packed and becoming very stuffy. Ossie, who was standing next to Herbie, began sniffing loudly and glancing down at Herbie's clothes. "Strewth, Herbie," he whispered. "Did you bring some of them pigs in here with you?"

Herbie's face turned bright red as the stink wafted up and no matter how he tried to ignore it seemed to get stronger. Very soon others were beginning to sniff loudly and glare in his direction. And, to add to his embarrassment, from the other side of the brick wall of the chapel there began a terrible squealing. Herbie groaned inwardly. He hadn't realised that the wall he had chosen to park the ute alongside was the back wall of the crematorium. Strewth, he thought to himself, I got to get out of here.

But before he'd edged half way across the room there was another distraction. A banging and rattling at the door. He glanced quickly in that direction. A small black boot and a blue-coated arm were trying to force their way in. The chapel attendant had a look of desperation on his face as he tried to counter this new and unexpected affront to the dignity of the proceedings. He didn't seem to know whether to continue to barricade the door or let the invader in.

Herbie tried to shrink into anonymity. He knew who it was. He felt it an appropriate time to pray for his own deliverance rather than Cec's. But, no doubt owing to the increasing clamour from both sides of the chapel, God couldn't hear his prayers, so poor Herbie had to just cringe into the corner and endure.

Up in front the minister was also becoming increasingly agitated. He was beginning to miss his lines. Then, as another sudden crescendo of pig screeching penetrated the wall alongside him, he seemed to momentarily lose his balance and fall back against the button which automated the conveyor belt. Before anybody could do anything, the coffin containing old Cec's body began its irrevocable journey towards the curtains which hid the chute to the furnace. With the final commitments still to come, the poor minister had to increase the tempo of his delivery to an almost incomprehensible gallop.

Then, as if the whole affair had been orchestrated to perfection, the moment Cec's coffin disappeared through the curtains and the pigs' squealing reached a crescendo that would have done justice to the not so distant wailing of a thousand banshees, the small body of young Gaye burst through the doors, spilling an armful of decapitated flowers all over the chapel floor.

"My God," Herbie heard the man alongside him say. "She's been at the wreaths. What a bummer!"

Herbie didn't bother to answer. He struggled his way through the crowd, grabbed his daughter under one arm and took off for his ute.

By the time the rest of the mourners rounded the building at the corner of the car park all that could be seen or heard of Herbie and his menagerie of misfits was a light trail of drifting dust in the afternoon's sunlight and the fading shrieks of a porcine fury that seemed no longer to belong to this world...

It was Ossie Nichols who told Pat the barman all about Cec's funeral. "It'll be a while before Herbie Miles shows his face in this town," he smirked. "An' yer know what? His missus give birth to another baby daughter. If she's anythin' like that young Gaye I reckon Herbie might be tempted to strangle the little bugger when Florrie brings her back from the city hospital."

He drained his glass and shook his head a little sadly. "Strewth, what a rotten way to send poor old Cec off!"

Pat was polishing glasses and looking a little pensive when he answered. "Ah, I don't know about that, Ossie," he said. "I reckon meself Cec's only regret ud be he wasn't there to enjoy it hisself."

Finders Keepers

One Saturday evening on his way down to Cliff Randall's pub Rolly Hills noticed a dozer chain lying by the roadway where the week previous the wood-chippers had been at work. The chain was draped neatly over a tree stump by the big bend where the coast road turned north. It looked like it had been put there ready to load but whoever was supposed to do that had forgotten.

Now Rolly was a man familiar with dozers and dozer chains and he knew immediately a chain of such size and quality was worth at least two hundred dollars or better on the open market - certainly too valuable to be left where it was. He decided to stop and get a closer dekko. Rolly's home-spun philosophy on honesty was a simple one - what you spied unattended and without obvious title by a country roadside was as much yours as anyone else's. Especially if the chain was the leftover of a departed woodchipping gang. He wasn't particularly friendly towards the woodchippers because he felt their only interest in the district was to make a quick dollar and then piss off to wreak havoc elsewhere. So he made a quick decision. Under the dubious law of "Finders Keepers" that chain was his.

It was a very heavy chain but Rolly, being a man of considerable size and strength, managed to struggle the chain on to the back of his ute without too much trouble. Having pulled up the tarp cover to hide the chain from prying eyes, he continued on his way to the pub very contented with what he saw as a good night's work. In fact he was so jubilant about his lucky find that he, in an uncharacteristic display of recklessness, later confided in Cliff, the owner and manager of the pub.

"A real tow chain it is, Cliff old mate," he said when he got the chance to get Cliff's ear to himself. "An' you know them chippers, matey, careless bludgers that they are, I reckon they won't even miss it. But just in case, don't tell anyone, ay? I mean, so far as I'm concerned it's as much mine now as anyone's." He leaned forward across the bar and winked at Cliff to seal the confidence. "You know how it is."

Cliff certainly did know how it was. He touched the side of his nose as an acknowledgment. "Sure Rolly, you know me; I mind me own business." Rolly knew he didn't really have to ask Cliff to keep his trap shut because very early one morning a couple of years before, he had accidentally come upon Cliff and his two sons illegally dragging the river for bream. He had given them a friendly wave in the morning light as he passed, just close enough for them to recognise who it was that had caught them out, and far enough away to indicate a certain disinterest in the whole proceedings. It was something Rolly had kept to himself because he knew very well that a secret kept was a valuable bargaining point when and if it came to asking favours. Or, to put it more bluntly, he knew Cliff couldn't afford to dob him in even if he wanted to.

Later that night, a little inebriated and still chuffed with his good fortune, Rolly drove home. The sound of the chain clunking away in the back of his ute filled him with great cheer. His mind was already formulating how and where he was going to flog it. But not for a while. Let the heat die down first. He decided first thing in the morning he was going to bury the chain in the heap of other bits and pieces that he kept in his barn until he found a buyer. There it would look, he thought, in place as if it had always been there.

But, poor Rolly, when he went to unload the chain the following morning he was horrified to see that what he'd thought was the chain bouncing around in the back of his ute the previous night was nothing more than a few old car parts which had, last time he'd seen them, been decorating a corner of Cliff Randall's pub yard. Now Rolly was a man of considerable native cunning. He knew who had his chain and how they had swopped it for their own rubbish. Cliff must have worded his sons up to snitch the bloody thing while he was partaking of those few drinks the night before. He also knew that going back and confronting Cliff with the fact of its disappearance was useless. Cliff would simply deny all knowledge of it and point out, quite rightly, that he hadn't left the bar all night. Neither could Rolly, in the circumstances of its acquisition, complain to the local cop. There had to be another way of getting his just revenge and he was determined that was what he was going to do.

So, having thought the problem through to its full conclusion, Rolly once again turned up at Cliff's pub the follow Saturday night. He gave Cliff a big smile and just set about having another few quiet beers and chatting to all and sundry. This time it was Cliff who couldn't keep his mouth shut. Stealing a march on his old rival Rolly Hills, who was known widely as the district's smartest operator, should have been satisfaction enough but Cliff wanted more, he wanted to see his old rival squirm, yet there was Rolly acting like he was at peace with the whole flamin' universe.

Half an hour before closing time Cliff couldn't stand it any longer. He had to get some response, so he tried a more direct approach. He offered Rolly a large beer on the house. "I've had a good week with the tourists an' all, Rolly," he said as he pushed the beer across the counter. "Besides, I figure I owe you somethin'. I mean, you bein' a good customer an' all." As he said it Cliff couldn't quite disguise the triumph in his voice. "By the way," he asked, "how'd yer go with that dozer chain you found? Got a good price I suppose?"

Rolly shook his head. "No I bloody well didn't. An' I didn't because some rotten bugger thieved the bloody thing from right under me nose." He gave Cliff a penetrating stare for a moment or two before he added rather regretfully. "Old mate," he said, "I don't know what the world's comin' to. There just ain't no honesty any more!"

Cliff had a bit of a quiet grin at Rolly's insinuation and then said with exaggerated sympathy, "Strewth Rolly, what a bummer. Pinched it you say. Now that's real stiff."

Rolly gave a resigned sigh. "Ar, I suppose it don't matter all that much, old mate. I mean, yer win some an' yer lose some. That's the way it always seems to go with me."

Cliff pricked his ears up at that. It just wasn't like Rolly at all - to be so philosophical about being taken down. Rolly hated losing out on anything, yet here he was accepting his demise with the fortitude of J.C. himself. It just wasn't flamin' well healthy.

For his part, Rolly seemed oblivious of all but the froth around the rim of his glass as he continued his philosophical dissertation on winning and losing in a slow thoughtful voice. He could have been talking to Cliff, but then again he could have been talking to himself. "Though in this case," he said with some conviction, "I suppose yer could say it was in the reverse. More like yer lose some an' yer win some, I reckon."

By this time Cliff was really intrigued. But he was also a little nervous. Rolly seemed more than just philosophical about his loss now - there was a touch there, he suspected, of something a little more ominous.

"How exactly do you mean, Rolly?" he asked.

Rolly ordered another beer and didn't answer until he had taken his first sip. "Ar, just like I said, old matey, somethin' always seems to turn up to balance things out. Not that it has exactly yet, mind you, but I got a real strong feelin' that it will. I mean, I was only thinkin' that the other mornin' when I was out in the hills tryin' to bag a bunny before breakfast." Rolly waved his hand casually in the general direction of the hill behind the pub. "Not too far from here as a matter of fact. I do a lot of me thinkin' in the mornin's. The mind's clearer yer know."

Cliff was getting decidedly nervous as he glanced quickly in the general direction of Rolly's indiscriminate wave. He thought he had detected a slight gloating in Rolly's tone of voice.

"You were up the hill? Out there?"

Rolly's thoughts seemed far away. He had a kind of dreamy look in his eye as if he was out there again in the early morning trying to bag that fat little bunny. "Yeah, sure," he said finally. "About a mile up the old timber road there." Then, as if he had suddenly remembered where he was, his attention returned to Cliff. "Yeah, Cliff old mate ... an' d'you know what, a real funny thing happened to me up there on the hill that mornin'. Like I said I was just wanderin' around listenin' to the birds an' things when I suddenly come across this little hut hidden away in the scrub. I thought to meself, hullo, hullo, I wonder why someone's got a hut so far away from anywhere? I mean it didn't looked lived in or nothin', yet there was this well-worn track leadin' right up to it. Well, old matey, when I took a gander through the cracks in the boards I got quite a surprise, believe me. There was all this fishin' gear in there! Nets, cray pots, reels, lines, you name it. All inside tucked away nice and neat under bits of hessian. Y'know, not that I could see 'em clear - just a suspicion about the shape of things like. Y'know?"

But Cliff didn't know. He didn't have any exact idea what Rolly was on about but he was beginning to. He certainly knew a case of smug satisfaction when he saw it. It was shining blatantly in Rolly's eyes as he lifted his glass and took another sip. "Yeah," Rolly continued, "a whole heap of stuff there was, Cliff old matey. I'd say, at a quick guess-timate, about four hundred and forty-eight dollars worth on the open market."

Rolly downed the remainder of his beer then and smacked his lips with satisfaction. "Well," he said as he looked around the empty bar, "I can't stay here gabbin' all night, can I? I'd better be off. I promised the missus I'd take her fishin' tomorrow." A quick wave (and was it a smirk too?) and Rolly was gone through the door.

Cliff waited no longer than for the sound of Rolly's old ute to fade into the night before he sprang into action. He grabbed a torch, slammed the bar door closed behind him and galloped up the hill behind his pub to the hut where he and his sons kept all their illicit fishing gear, the nets he used to poach the river, the pots he used to poach the crays. Sure enough when he finally got there his worst fears were realised. The place was cleaned out. There wasn't one single hook or bit of salted bait left.

Naturally enough as he slumped back down the hill his mind was full of vengeance. "That bastard Rolly," he kept repeating to himself. "That bastard, he pinched all me gear, and sold the bloody lot for a miserable four hundred and forty-eight dollars."

And he still hadn't got one cent out of that lousy dozer chain.

A Favour Given
is a Favour Returned

Ossie Nichols' farm was the steepest farm in the district. As someone once said, "When yer walk Ossie's farm an' you ain't goin' up then yer comin' down."

But the farm's saving grace was its fertility. "The best chocolate soil in the world," Ossie was often heard to boast. Which was a slight exaggeration seeing Ossie hadn't seen a lot of the rest of the world. Nevertheless, hilly or not, anyone who had clapped eyes on Ossie's lush spring pastures never failed to be impressed. Consequently Ossie tried to work every inch of his ground and to do that he had to plough almost half of his acreage with horses. So it wasn't surprising when he also used to boast that he knew as much about horses as anyone in the district. Which wasn't really much of a boast seeing most farmers in the district had given up horses long ago. Though, as it turned out, he didn't know everything about the subject. It had taken a man who knew nothing about them to prove that.

It happened the time when Ossie's big roan lead horse Roany died suddenly of a heart attack going up one of those hills. Because he was only half way through his autumn ploughing Ossie found it necessary to get an immediate replacement. Though how he was going to replace such a fine old horse he didn't know.

Until, that was, Ron Saw the butcher mentioned that he'd heard the Jones' farm would soon be on the market. Ron explained that Kingsley Jones had spread it about that since his dad old Cec had gone to those evergreen pastures in the sky, he felt no obligation to keep the farm going. He didn't intend to bust his gut all his life like his old man had, evergreen pastures waiting or not. Kingsley made it plain to all and sundry around the town that he intended to sell the property and with the money realise his life's ambition of setting up a fish and chip shop in one of the nearby coastal towns.

Because the Jones' farm was the only other farm in the district that still used horses Ossie saw his chance to get a satisfactory replacement for old Roany. If Kingsley Jones was going to sell his farm he wasn't going to want his father's team of horses and Ossie knew them to be good ones, especially the lead horse. Unfortunately for Ossie by the time he caught up with Kingsley he was too late. Rolly Hills, it seemed, had also heard the rumour and come to the same conclusion as Ossie. He had already arranged to buy both horses from Kingsley Jones for a client in another town.

Now Ossie reckoned Rolly still owed him a favour. Hadn't he nursed a sick boar for Rolly the winter before last? He decided it was worth a try to appeal to Rolly's good nature to secure the horse for himself. He rang Rolly and put it to him.

But Rolly's good nature, it seemed, didn't run to commercial transactions. He told Ossie he couldn't let him have either of the horses because he'd already promised them to another farmer up the coast. "If I break up the pair I'll be breakin' me word," Rolly told him. "You know how it is, matey."

"Okay," Ossie said. "I'll give you thirty bucks more than you paid Kingsley for the lead horse."

"Make it fifty an' yer on," Rolly replied succinctly. "I reckon it's worth at least that much to talk me client out of it."

Ossie was pretty certain Rolly didn't have any such deal going. He well knew that Rolly couldn't have afforded to welsh on any deal for a mere fifty dollars. But he also knew that if he really wanted that horse he was going to have to pay the extra money.

"Okay, Rolly," he said finally. "But just don't come askin' me for any more favours, ay."

"Would I ever?" Rolly asked in a rather aggrieved tone. And just in case Ossie wanted to argue about it he quickly told Ossie he could pick up the horse from Kingsley as soon as he wanted and banged down the phone.

The following day Ossie arrived on foot at the Jones' farm to collect the horse. Kingsley was quite surprised to see he had come without a truck.

"I told Rolly he'd need a truck to shift him," Kingsley said. "That horse was born an' bred on this farm and he's never been off it. I don't reckon he'll take too kindly to bein' led away. The trouble is he's a bit stubborn. If he don't like somethin' he takes a hell of a lot of persuadin'. Get yourself a truck's my advice."

...you very seldom saw Mrs Morgan because if she wasn't washing she was cooking ...

Ossie didn't want any advice. Hadn't he been around horses since he was a boy? He knew all about stubborn horses. He assumed it was more likely that Kingsley, who had a name in the district for being a bit of a drongo, didn't know what he was talking about. It was Ossie's creed that if a horse was hard to handle it was more than likely due to the handler than it was the horse. Even his old Roany had been a bit stubborn when he was younger. Besides, he reckoned he'd already paid too much for the new horse and certainly wasn't going to spend more hiring a truck. "Don't you worry about it. I'll walk him home okay," he told Kingsley. "It'll give me the chance ter get to know him."

Half an hour later he led the big brown draught horse down the road towards the township and in spite of Kingsley's doubts the horse didn't seem to have any objections at all about being taken away from his spiritual home. "Yer just got to talk to 'em in the right voice," he told Kingsley who had accompanied him to the first bend in the road. "Show 'em who's boss from the very start an' they'll respond."

At first it seemed as though Ossie's philosophy was sound. The horse clopped happily behind him all the way down the hill from the Jones' farm and right through the main street of the town. But that was as good as it got. The moment they came to the road leading up to Ossie's farm, the brown horse suddenly decided he had gone far enough. He propped right where he was and wouldn't be shifted no matter how hard Ossie tugged at the lead strap.

Being an old hand at the business, Ossie wasn't too much perplexed. He simply undid the flap of the satchel he was carrying and took out one of the turnips he had been saving for just such an occasion. He gave the horse one good bite at it and then held the remainder of the turnip just beyond the horse's reach. When the horse moved forward for a second bite, Ossie moved the turnip away again. In that manner Ossie managed to coax the horse up the road step by step. But it was tiring work and at the corner of the first big bend Ossie decided to take a rest. He tied the horse to a fence post and sat down in the shade of a tree. As fortune would have it, the place he chose to stop was right alongside Lester Morgan's house.

Lester, who was a fireman with the railways, was doing a bit of digging in his vegie garden before he was due to leave for his afternoon shift. Lester had a very large vegie garden because he had a very large family to feed. Whenever you passed the house the two clothes lines were likely to be weighted down with clothes drying. And if you looked carefully enough at the gradation of clothing from largest to smallest, you could almost work out how many kids there were in the family and how old they were.

Neither were those lines ever completely free of nappies. It was said in the township that you very seldom saw Mrs Morgan because if she wasn't washing she was cooking and if she wasn't cooking she and Lester were procreating. Anyway, the moment Lester saw Ossie appear, he dived inside his house and came out a few moments later carrying a long glass of cold fruit juice which he offered to Ossie.

Now Lester (as it has already been demonstrated) was a friendly little bloke but he had an affliction, he had a terrible stutter. What took the average person only a few seconds to say could often take Lester several minutes. And sometimes, when he really got excited, he had been known to dry up completely. It wasn't at all the kind of trait that endeared him to busy people, and that day Ossie, who knew all about Lester's affliction, considered one way or another he was pretty damn busy. He wasn't going to be suckered into a marathon listening session with Lester while there was a stubborn horse to be got home. Neither was he going to speak in case it encouraged Lester to do the same. So, he downed the fruit juice with a series of nods, grunts and in-between smiles, hoping as he returned the empty glass to Lester it would convey to him the kind of mute g'day, thanks, and see-yer-later combination he intended.

But Lester wasn't interested in such subtleties. He hurriedly tossed the empty glass into the long grass and began clambering through the fence, his mouth already shaping and reshaping the words as he prepared himself for his next bout with the English language. There also seemed to be some kind of urgent intention in his swirling hands as he confronted Ossie directly. As if, Ossie thought, he was cranking up to a full head of steam.

"S-s-s-s-a-a-a-a-y O-o-o-o-ss-ie wh-wh-wh-why d-d-d-d-on't y-y-y-y-you..."

As if the stubborn horse wasn't enough Ossie now had Lester to deal with. He gave his benefactor a final smile of thanks and prepared to continue on his way up the hill. But no way was Ossie getting his drink for nothing. Lester had something to say and he seemed determined to get it out. "B-b-b-u-u-t wh-wh-wh-wh..."

"It's okay Les," Ossie kept insisting. "Tell me later. I've got to get this horse home."

What with the tubby little fireman alongside him, urgently struggling for the words that wouldn't come, and the horse near on dragging his arm off, Ossie found the going even more difficult as he advanced step by step up the dusty road. It took him almost as long to get the horse up the short hill above Lester's house as it had getting him right across town. He also ran out of turnips and he still wasn't even half way home. He decided it was time for another rest. He tied the horse to a sapling by the road and sat down on the bank fanning his face with his hat.

"Wouldn't mind that drink now, Les," he said with a wry smile. Not quite defeated but nearly so.

Lester stood there, hands on hips, looking at him with a kind of sad, unfulfilled look. Pained even. "W-w-w-hy d-d-don-t y-y-y-ou g-git b-behind h-him an' d-drive h-h-im Ossie, w-was w-what I was tryin' to say. He m-might go better." Lester said it this time almost with ease. It was as if the getting to the top of the hill had done away with the urgency and it had suddenly all popped out.

Ossie stared at Lester for a second or two and then he nodded. He would have been willing by that time to take advice from the Devil himself. "Okay Les," he said suddenly, "thanks for the advice. You could be right. I reckon it's worth a try. A bit of a whack on his rump might do the trick."

He stood up and carefully folded the halter over the back of the horse's neck then he turned and gave Lester the nod. "Seein' it's your idea, Les, you have first whack an' we'll see what happens."

Without hesitation Lester bent down, picked up a sturdy stick lying by the roadside, and then with one loud "h-ha" he brought the stick down on the horse's rump with all the strength he could muster.

"Strewth!" Ossie yelled as the horse leaped forward with such power it nearly ripped his arms from out of their sockets. He let go the halter with a short cry of pain, and the horse, taking his yell as a prelude to the next painful whack, leaped forward again; only this time instead of heading up the road, he slewed sideways and headed for the roadside fence which he took in one gigantic bound. In no time at all the horse disappeared into thick scrub, heading Ossie surmised miserably, back down the hill in the general direction of his old home.

When the sounds of the bolting horse finally faded, Ossie turned to his would-be helper. His voice was repressed but undeniably wrathful. "Bloody hell, Lester," he said, "when I said whack, I didn't mean for yer to break his bloody back!"

And poor Lester who once again could see he had ruined the possibility of a meaningful friendship, hung his head, turned on his heel and walked slowly and despondently back down the road without a backward glance. Ossie watched him go, wordless himself now, glaring after the retreating figure. Then, giving the day up as a bad job, he spat into the dust and headed in the opposite direction towards his farm, cursing horses and stutterers with equal intensity each angry stride he took.

The following morning the little fireman was again in his vegie garden as the cattle truck with Ossie's new horse on board drove slowly up the road. Ossie was sitting alongside the driver. When he spotted Lester he motioned the driver to stop. He got down from the cab and strolled across to the house fence. "G'day, Les," he called. "How are yer today?"

Still conscious of his poor showing the previous day, and not quite knowing what to expect, Lester lowered the hoe he had been weeding his potatoes with and gave Ossie a tentative nod. He certainly wasn't going to attempt to say anything.

"Seein' as how things ended yesterday," Ossie said, "I thought it only decent to thank yer for yer trouble. I mean it was rude of me to storm off like I did. Later, when I got to thinkin' about it, I began to feel a bit ashamed. I mean, I know yer was only tryin' to help me with me problem. So I thought ... well, a favour given's a favour returned, ay." Ossie stopped then and smiled at Lester expansively. "An' yer know what Les? I come up with this great idea that might help you with yer stutterin'."

Lester brightened up considerably when he heard that, and perhaps because he was more relaxed, he managed to get the question out without too much difficulty. "W-w-wh-at's t-t-th-at O-o-ossie?"

Ossie smiled benignly across at him. "Well," he said, "it's like this, Les - the next time yer want to give advice about horses to an expert on horses - don't. Better all round to keep yer trap closed, I reckon." With that said Ossie tipped his hat grandly and walked back to the truck.

As they drove off up the road towards his farm he turned to the driver with a satisfied grin. "I wonder just how long it'll take old Lester to tell me to get st-stuffed, ay?" he said.

A Private Kind of Humour

Old Willum Haas was an aloof sort of bloke and not very popular with the locals. He didn't belong to any farmer organisations - or for that matter any other kind of organisation, committee, club or group. Some had tried from time to time to include Willum and his wife Hilda in various social occasions over the years but all their well-meant efforts had failed dismally. Old Willum always had an elaborate excuse why they couldn't come.

It was a rare event even for Willum or his missus to set foot in the town's shopping centre. It was said that the pair of them truly lived off the land; most of what they ate they grew on their rough little hill farm. Other essentials were bought in bulk from the city and picked up by Willum at the Montvale railway station, either early in the morning on his way to a ploughing or dozing job, or late in the evening when he was on his way home. All that most saw of Willum was a quick glimpse of him through the window of his beat-up old Fargo truck as he carted his equally beat-up old machinery from one job to another.

His wife Hilda, who was generally considered to be a few sheep short of a flock, was seen even less. As one local wit once said: "There's some bin born, lived an' died in this here district that's never clapped eyes on old Hilda Haas." And by the way it was said it was easy enough to draw the inference that this was a positive, rather than a negative, fact.

Anyway, it wasn't just old Willum's lack of interest in district matters that caused animosity. The main accusation was a more specific one. There were still those who could remember the terrible drought in the late sixties when old Willum was the only farmer who had refused to support the combined "Prayers for Rain" services conducted by the three main churches. The reason he gave for this rejection was he hadn't made up his mind whether he wanted rain or not.

Willum took pains to point out the problem to the pair of organisers who had waylaid him in the township at the time. He told them that even though the big dry was bad for his farm, it was good for his dozer work which, during the protracted drought, mainly involved pushing up clay fill dams in the expectation for an eventual change in the weather. He directed the organisers' attention to the sky above with his finger, indicating to them the indecisive nature of the ragged clouds and sporadic sunshine when he made his point. "It all seems so confused," he told them. Though whether he was referring to the battle between sun and cloud or his own state of mind he didn't say. "I jus' thought I'd leave it up to God to decide what to do. I wouldn't want to try and influence Him, I wouldn't."

To a person the residents of the district were incensed. They had no objection to a man making a quid or two but this was beyond the pale. It smacked, they grumbled, of greed and selfishness. Of course they did continue to employ Willum to do their rough ploughing and the bit of hay baling the drought allowed because he was a fair bit cheaper than any other contractor but, nevertheless, the name 'piker' stuck and old Willum was voted the most unpopular man in the district.

As always there were many conflicting views why he was so difficult to get along with. Phylis Barnes the baker's wife, always reckless in her estimations of others' weaknesses, reckoned old Willum's sourness was due to an excess of bile in his system. "It's the food they eat up on that miserable little farm of theirs that's the problem," she told any who had the time or interest to listen. "Too much red meat and spuds. They eat nothin' else, you know."

Harold Bushell was one who scoffed at such a suggestion. "C'mon Phylis," he told her. "Talkin' red meat down in a farmin' district is nothin' short of heresy. You're only gripin' because they don't buy yer old man's bread. I reckon it ain't so much what they don't eat as what they don't drink. The Haas' are teetotallers yer know, an' I never yet seen a happy teetotaller."

A Private Kind of Humour

And so it went on. It seemed just about everyone in the district had their own pet reason for Willum's lugubrious nature. Even Rolly Hills, who usually didn't bother to engage in local gossip, had his own version of Willum's problem. His explanation was direct and simple. "It's because both Willum's parents were Germans," he insisted. "Everyone knows that the Germans take life very serious. A German with a sense of humour is rarer than yer illusive Tassie tiger."

In fact it seemed the only person who constantly stuck up for old Willum was Nola Prate. It was her contention that old Willum's humour was misunderstood. She often took Rolly to task over it. "You're not entirely wrong, Rolly," she told him once when he had popped in about afternoon tea time and launched into his current favourite subject of slandering old Willum.

"Your trouble is, Rolly, you're only seein' it from a racist viewpoint," she said. "It isn't that he's got no humour, it's because it's a different kind of humour - a kind of humour that's a bit like himself - kind of private."

Rolly wasn't letting her get away with that. "Ar, the trouble with you, Nola, is yer just won't see what's right under yer eyes. What about the time the silly old coot was ploughin' for the Colonel with an alarm clock strapped to the dashboard of his cat tractor. When the Colonel's foreman asked him why he din' wear a wristlet watch like everyone else old Willum tol' him it was because he couldn't hear a wristlet watch. I mean if that ain't crazy I don't know what is."

Nola shrugged. "If you was ploughin' for the Colonel how would you do it, Rolly?"

It was Rolly's turn to shrug. "As quick as I could I reckon. So's I could get off the place."

"Sure you would, an' you'd lose money," Nola retorted. "No, Rolly, there's only one way to plough for a rich man, an' that's just as good and as fast as he expects. Old Willum's been ploughin' the Colonel's paddocks for years now an' I'll bet you my best dairy cow to a packet of peanuts he knows exactly how fast he's got to go to keep the Colonel happy. That alarm clock's probably part of some elaborate system he's made up to measure acres per hour or somethin'. You mark my words, Rolly."

Rolly laughed derisively. "Ar, come off the grass, Nola - that's a bit fanciful ain't it?"

"Is it, Rolly? Well I'll tell you somethin' else that might change your mind. Last summer when old Willum did my balin', the engine of that rickety bit of old rubbish he calls a baler kept cuttin' out. D'know how he'd fix it? He'd get down from his tractor, take off his old hat real casual like, spit at nothin' in particular, then he'd hop inter that engine with his hat and whale the livin' daylights out of it. After that he'd climb back onto his tractor an' give the starter button a press. That darn old contraption would start up as easy as you like. I saw him do that many times an' never once did he fail to get it goin' again."

Rolly couldn't help smirking openly. "Yer reckon that's bright do yer, Nola?"

Nola ignored his sarcasm. "No Rolly, but as it happened the thing stopped once when Willum didn't think I was watchin' an' that time he just sat there for a couple of minutes rollin' himself a cigarette. When he was finished he lent over an' pressed the starter button with exactly the same result. I figured he was just lettin' the engine cool down a bit. All that beltin' an' carry on was for my benefit not the engine's. I reckon it's all show. I reckon it's old Willum's way of copin' with boredom!"

By this time Rolly was getting a little pissed off with Nola making excuses for someone he knew to be a right old coot so he decided to bring the matter to a head. He tossed good sense to the winds. "Okay, Nola," he said, "I'll tell yer what I'll do, I'll bet you right here an' now one whole week's work out of young Tom an' me to a batch of yer date scones that one day Willum'll do somethin' so stupid it'll prove once an' for all he's as silly as a square wheel! Are yer on?"

Nola gave him another knowing smile. In her mind she was sure she was right and that Rolly would come to rue the day he had made such a rash bet. "We'll see," she said. She got up and walked to the oven. "Meanwhile, I'm sure you wouldn't mind tryin' one or two of those date scones right now, ay Rolly?"

Neither Rolly nor Nola could have predicted just how soon the subject matter of the bet would again be raised. In fact hardly a month had gone by before it was on with a vengeance. According to a rumour that was doing the rounds old Willum had a right run in with the local quack who had taken up the position as local doctor a couple of years before.

Shortly after his arrival in the district it was realised by the locals that he wasn't there for their benefit so much as he was to escape what he called "the abominable National Health Scheme in Britain where a doctor was just another cog in the machine."

The new doctor hadn't much liked settling into a district so far removed from civilisation but had decided to do so because he couldn't afford anything better. It was, he had once confessed to his small circle of friends, an unavoidable durance he would have to suffer in his pursuit of eventual comfort and riches.

Of course, he didn't actually say it as bluntly as that, but that was what he meant. And in truth it was a reasonably easy practice to run - a couple of hours in the surgery six days a week and the occasional and unavoidable house call, which from the beginning he'd made it his business to discourage. The rest of his time was taken up pursuing his twin life-time passions for growing roses and playing golf.

Consequently, when late on one of those kind of stormy nights in the district when even the lowliest of fools knew the simple act of nicking out for another log of wood from the woodshed was fraught with all kinds of danger, the Doc received an urgent call from old Willum Haas telling him that Mrs Haas had taken a real bad turn, the Doc's immediate reaction was to insist old Willum bring Mrs Haas down to the surgery. "It would be easier for you to bring your wife down in your truck than for me to go up there in my car," he told Willum.

But old Willum wasn't going to be persuaded by such a reasonable plea. At the other end of the phone he seemed to be in danger of taking some kind of bad turn himself. "Gawd Doc, I wouldn't dare. She's pretty crook, she is. If she got wet..."

Willum left the consequences of that particular scenario up in the air. Then, while the Doc was still searching for other reasonable excuses not to go, Willum's urgent voice again crackled down the phone. "Gawd Doc, she's findin' it hard to breathe, she is, an' I think she's turnin' blue."

The Doc finally gave up. He didn't want to go, not at all, but he did have an obligation to his Hippocratic oath. The tone of his response, therefore, was couched halfway between tiresome duty and personal condescension. "Right, Mr Haas, try not to panic. I'll be there as soon as possible. Meanwhile keep your wife warm and quiet. There's a good man."

As it turned out "as soon as possible" was quite a while. Getting up the narrow dirt road to the Haas' farm in broad daylight was challenge enough; on a dark and stormy night when an equinox gale was trying to blow the knot holes out of the iron-bark fence posts, such a journey was akin to Scott's fateful attempt to reach the South Pole.

In fact it took the Doc nearly two hours to get there. The bucketing rain from the north-east had turned every creek and culvert into a raging torrent. And just to aggravate matters the local council had also done their bit to thwart the Doc's attempt to administer medical largesse to Mrs Haas by spreading a nice thick coating of yellow dirt (which had now become slippery yellow mud) in anticipation of the spring deluges.

To continue on his way the Doc had to forsake the relative comfort of his car and struggle ankle deep in wet mud to fix skid chains to the back wheels. And then around the very next bend he nearly ran right into a tree that had come down across the road.

Fortunately for the Doc, two years experience in such an unpredictable climate had taught him the efficacy of carrying a chainsaw in the boot. With the vision of Mrs Haas' blue face and choking breath before him, he clambered out of his car again and hopped into the branches of that fallen tree like a man possessed.

Once he had the road cleared he thought his mercy dash would be accomplished with ease. But it wasn't as simple as that. He hadn't counted on Willum's three rickety old farm gates, and all three of them closed. Not surprisingly, by the time he got to the farm house he had been soaked through so many times the only purpose his wet-weather gear served was to hold the cold wetness in.

Old Willum met him at the door and led him through an unbelievably cluttered kitchen, down a long empty echoing hallway lined with scrim and paper and into a small dark bedroom which seemed entirely filled by a huge brass and iron bed. Sitting in the middle of the bed, propped up in a pile of apricot-coloured lace-edged pillows, was Hilda Haas. She was wearing a bright purple dressing gown with a fluffy white ruff done up tightly at the neck. Pulled down over her head was a red and white striped woollen beanie. There were old magazines and chocolate wrappers liberally scattered all over the pink chenille bedspread. Her face, in spite of Willum's earlier claim, was bright red, not blue. She looked, the Doc thought, not unlike an antipodean facsimile of Charles Dickens' Mrs Micawber.

The Doc gave a heavy sigh and opened his little black bag. He pulled out his stethoscope and waggled it rather imperiously in the old lady's direction. "I'll just have to ask you to loosen the neck of your dressing gown, Mrs Haas," he said.

But rather than comply with the Doc's reasonable request Mrs Haas flung both her hands up to her neck. "Not on yer life," she said. "Not in front of a stranger."

The Doc was a little bewildered. He tried to keep his voice calm. "But Mrs Haas," he said, "I'm the doctor and I've come all this way on this terrible night just to examine you."

Hilda Haas pointed a dramatic finger towards old Willum who was still skulking in the doorway. "It wasn't me who asked you to come," she said in a cracked accusing voice. "It was him! He's worried I mightn't be well enough to cook his flamin' breakfast tomorra."

Old Willum hurried away then and left the Doc to examine Mrs Haas the best way he could.

Later in the kitchen the Doc gave Willum his heated and candid diagnosis of Hilda's illness. "Nothing worse than a heavy cold," he told Willum sternly. "Nothing that a few days in bed won't cure."

He forbore to say that after his own night's endeavour he envisaged himself coming down with a similar complaint. "For goodness sake, man," he continued as he prepared to leave, "you could have easily bundled her into your truck and taken her down to my surgery. It would have saved me a two hour trek up this little track they call a road in this God-forsaken country."

The story goes, that rather than take umbrage at the Doc's chastisement, old Willum had cocked his ear as a fresh gust of rain and wind shook the dilapidated farm house. He answered the Doc finally in a hurt aggrieved voice. "Ar, come off it Doc." he said. "Yer couldn't ask a man ter go out on a night like this, yer couldn't."

It was never recorded what the Doc's reply was, which is a shame, but it was later told by Willum's nearest neighbour Billy Gernhart that he heard the Doc's car departing that night in a very dangerous manner and the following morning Willum had complained to him that the Doc had not even bothered to close his three gates in spite of his newly purchased "Shut The Bloody Gate" signs.

When Rolly Hills heard about it he lost no time in carrying the news back to Nola. In her kitchen he told her the sad story. "The old dill's finally proved my point like I said he would," he told Nola. "Did yer ever hear of anythin' so stupid? I reckon if the quack had killed him right there an' then it wouldn't have gone beyond the bounds of his hippercritic oath. Even if old Willum falls into his baler and chops himself into little pieces the Doc ain't gonner do nothin' about it. Old Willum's done himself in good an' proper I'd say."

As it happened Nola wasn't all that moved by Rolly's triumphant declaration. She gave him a knowing smile and then moved across to where the iron kettle was singing away on the combustion stove. As she poured the boiling water into the teapot she said over her shoulder, "I suppose you wouldn't say no to a cuppa, Rolly, an' one or two of your favourite date scones?"

Rolly could hardly contain his glee. He sat at the kitchen table rubbing his hands together in anticipation. "You've conceded then?" he said.

Unhurriedly Nola poured the tea as she answered. "As a matter of fact I haven't, Rolly; but then I don't necessarily disagree with you either when you say the Doc won't treat old Willum or Hilda again."

She pushed the plate of scones under Rolly's nose. "You see," she said, "it seems like I've heard the other news an' you haven't."

Even though there wasn't the tiniest hint of a smirk in her expression when she said it Rolly suspected it wasn't too far away. His initial warm glow of triumph was already fading. "Ar, c'mon Nola, out with it," he demanded.

A Private Kind of Humour

"Well," Nola said, "as you probably know, the Doc's favourite patient and confidant Colonel Foote has a dicky heart, so the Doc's been treatin' him regular ever since he's been in the district. As it happens I was over at the Colonel's place just this mornin' and I'm telling you Rolly, he's a very worried man - 'cause the Doc's leavin' you see - in a week or so. He's bought inter a medical practice in the city. An', as you probably also know, old Willum's been ploughing for the Colonel all month - so I reckon he would have heard the news too, don't you reckon?"

To say the least Rolly was flabbergasted. But he wasn't going to give up without a fight. "Ar, c'mon Nola, nobody'd go that far just for a laugh. You're havin' me on!"

Nola grinned at him across the kitchen table. "Well Rolly, as you often say yourself, Willum's an unpredictable old devil. Who knows what he might do? An' even though I reckon it's slightly weighed in my favour I do at least concede neither of us will ever know the real truth of the matter, so I won't hold you to your bet."

Rolly was still scowling as he hoed into the plate of hot date scones. He had a nasty feeling he'd been conned somewhere down the line but kept reminding himself that even if he had won that bloody bet it wouldn't have turned out much different. He ate half a dozen scones that afternoon but later, when he came to think about it, they really hadn't tasted as good as usual.

Bonfire Night

The district's Annual Agriculture Show was held each year on the second Saturday of January, the time of year when most of the hay harvest was safely tucked up in the farm barns and the early season's veg crops were flourishing.

The day of the show that year had been unusually hot for the Montvale district so where better to hold a post-mortem of the day's events than the cool public bar of Conolly's pub. Who won what, who didn't - that kind of thing. And to the observant eye it wasn't difficult to pick the winners from the losers by their expressions in the bar that night - the winners, generous in their success, trying not to smile too much and the losers doing their best to smile at everything.

Halfway through the evening Donny Conolly the publican came into the main bar to see if Pat the barman wanted any help. Pat shook his head. "No, boss," he said, "things were a bit lively earlier but now they seem to have settled down a bit. There ain't a lot of drinkin' goin' on. There seems more losers slowly drownin' their sorrows than winners recklessly celebratin' their success."

He was about to suggest to his boss that a free round might liven things up a bit when the unusually hushed atmosphere in the bar was suddenly shattered by the strident clamour of the town's fire-bell outside in the main street. Inevitably, all the time-worn jokes about who had forgotten to damp down the dairy fire or turn their electric stoves off began to fly around. But other than that predictable response, the sound of the fire-bell's strident ring caused no real alarm because it was assumed that it simply heralded another late burn-off that had got away.

It was, therefore, quite a shock to those in the pub when the town's fire warden Harvey Stone and the police sergeant charged into the public bar with the news that one of Colonel Foote's open hay barns was on fire. "An' the bloody fire-truck won't start," Harvey shouted. "If we can't get water to the stack it'll be a gonna for sure."

Next it was the sergeant's turn to savour the drama. He positioned himself on the small raised platform next to the dilapidated old piano and addressed all those present in a loud and urgent voice. "Harvey an' me thought you lot might be willin' to lend a hand. We thought perhaps we could get a bucket chain goin' from the creek. The rest of the fire crew's collectin' all the buckets they can find. What do you reckon fellers? Are you willin' to give it a go?"

Even though the Colonel wasn't the most popular man in the district, and some of those present might even have got some quiet enjoyment out of the news that one of his hay stacks was on fire, most of the drinkers readily volunteered their aid. The current local topic had just about been exhausted anyway. The general feeling seemed to be that a new bit of excitement wouldn't go amiss.

The only person who didn't seemed to be getting fired up was Donny Conolly who watched with increasing mortification as the bar began to rapidly clear of his patrons. Hands on hips, he just stood there behind the bar with the kind of vacant disbelieving stare of a man who had just missed the last train to Paradise.

"Our best Saturday night of the year gone down the chute," he said later to Pat as he gazed around the almost empty bar. "Just like that silly old bugger the Colonel to let his hay catch fire. He always was in a tearin' hurry to get it under cover, an' always before it's properly dry. Half-cured hay just bursts into flames. Internal combustion they call it."

Pat, who knew more about those kind of things than his city-bred boss, didn't bother to correct him. "Yeah," he said rather regretfully. "What a shame."

But Pat's regret was more to do with not being able to join in the fun. He stood by the window watching the cavalcade of vehicles as they followed the blue flashing lights of the police car down the main street in the direction of the Colonel's property. What with all the noise of the revving engines, the tooting of horns, the fumes rising and the excited bustle as the pub's ex-patrons poured themselves into any available transport, it could have been a dramatic film he was watching. "Yeah, boss," he repeated as he wandered around picking up the scattered, hastily emptied glasses without his usual enthusiasm. "What a bloody shame."

... the winners trying not to smile too much; the losers doing their best to smile at everything.

Fortunately for the Colonel there was very little wind that evening and the haystack was not the raging inferno it could have been. It took no time at all for Harvey to organise a human bucket brigade from the burning stack to the nearby creek and within half an hour the fire was well under control. From that time on it was just a matter of waiting around to make sure there were no other outbreaks.

The Colonel, true to his character, spent most of his time and energy countermanding Harvey's orders and insisting those at the front end of the chain took care not to spoil the unburnt hay bales. Young Tommy Wright, who was high up under the roof and doing most of the throwing, resented the Colonel's inference. He had suffered similar disparagement in the past in the short time he had worked for the Colonel and didn't see why he should have to put up with it now. "If he don't put a sock in it, I'll have to do somefink abart it one way or another," he told Harvey Stone.

"Don't worry about him," Harvey said. "I'm the boss here, you just do as I say." He passed young Tommy another bucket and pointed to a spot where the smoke was still trickling up from some bales under the open roof. "Hit the roof with it, Tommy, an' let it spray back. That should take the heat out of the timber for a bit."

Young Tommy took a deep breath and swung the bucket of water high in the air. Perhaps his foot slipped, perhaps it didn't. No-one was game to bet on it, really. All they knew was the bucket seemed to slew around at the last second and instead of the water hitting the fire-blackened rafters it hit the Colonel, who was still shouting orders from the sidelines, fair in the face. It certainly shut him up that night and naturally enough the Colonel wasn't too happy with his unexpected dousing. Especially in view of the fact that the water coming down the chain was, to say the least, becoming decidedly muddy.

But to give him his due he did manage to treat the whole incident with some jocularity. He even referred to it later when he stood up on the blackened heap of burnt hay and gave his speech of thanks. "Ladies and gentlemen," he said, in the same kind of pedantic voice he used for his after dinner Rotary speeches, "it has been a hot dry job we have accomplished this night ... (Pause) ... although, in my case, not so hot as I have been somewhat unexpectedly cooled. (Pause again for laughter). However, I am grateful for the effort you have all put in here and, as a small mark of my appreciation, I thought we might return to the place from whence you came ... and this time it will be my shout."

Young Tommy, who was still hyped up about dousing his old enemy with a bucket full of dirty water, saw his chance to get another one back on the Colonel. "Good on yer, Colonel," he yelled. "Did you hear that, mateys, the Colonel's goin' to buy us a barrel. Three cheers for the Colonel."

By the time the cheering faded the deal seemed sealed and if anyone saw the Colonel's furious scowl in young Tommy's direction nobody bothered to mention it. They were too busy hurrying back to their various transport. The most important thing on the agenda now was to get back to Conolly's pub as quickly as possible to ensure a good possie by the bar where they could do justice to that promised barrel...

The remainder of that night went off without a hitch. It was well after closing time when the sergeant managed to exert his authority enough to begin the task of sending all the revellers home. "C'mon, c'mon, fair go. You lot'll get me sacked if you don't all go home."

Though in truth the reason the sergeant wasn't all that dedicated to closing down the pub that night might have been disclosed when Jeanie Spratt the bootmaker's wife pointed out to her group of confidants that up until that time the sergeant had been sitting in one of the out of the way corners in the company of Phylis Barnes from the bakery. "An' we all know about Phylis, don't we," she said with a broad wink as she passed her glass to Pat for a refill. "Ever since she was caught behind the bike shed in primary school she's been at it. I don't know why that poor husband of hers puts up with it."

She gave a quick look around then, not so much to see if anyone was eavesdropping as it was to establish the importance of her next piece of information. "I mean there was that little unexplained incident at the fire when the sergeant and Phylis couldn't be found, wasn't there? He was supposed to be organisin' the bucket brigade wasn't he. 'Everyone has to be relieved every ten minutes,' he said. Then next minute when I looked around he was gone."

She sniffed then and gave a triumphant smirk. "I wonder what kind of relief he was givin' Phylis. You mark my words, tonight's little episode is festerin' into the town's next big scandal."

One way or another that unexpected bonfire night continued to be the major talking point for several days. It certainly beat talking about the relative merits of Amy Pike's jams, Ossie Nichols' potatoes,

Denny Bourke's porkers and the Colonel's pedigree bulls. But you can only stretch a good thing so far and it wasn't too long before the stories going around were getting rather thin. Consequently on the following Saturday night the amount of life and chatter in the bar was about as much as you'd expect from a dead bandicoot. So much so that Donny Conolly came in from the dining room a little after eight o'clock, as he had on the Saturday night previous, to enquire of Pat what the problem was.

"I dunno, boss," Pat said. "It's a funny sort of night - everyone seems a bit bored, or edgy maybe. Some of 'em have been sittin' over their drinks for near on half an hour at a time. The place reminds me of a bloody bus station. You know, like they don't want to get another drink in case the bus arrives before they've time to finish it."

It was an astute observation on Pat's part for no sooner had he said it when, like the Saturday before, the quiet atmosphere in the pub was again shattered by the strident clanging of the fire bell from the street outside. Within seconds the bar was cleared. Donny Conolly looked at Pat, his flushed face registering first puzzlement, then a dawning disbelief. "Christ all mighty, Pat, they wouldn't dare, would they?"

Before Pat could answer, an excited George Saw poked his head back round the bar-room door. "Hey you blokes," he called. "Th' boys suggested you might get a fresh barrel up. You know - jus' in case." Then he was gone.

From outside in the street they could already hear the clamour of many voices shouting, orders being given, engines starting up. Pat answered finally, "I wouldn't bet on it boss. That fire truck's still under repair, so I hear."

Flash

Rolly Hills turned up at Harold Bushell's farm one morning. Harold had just finished milking and was heading back to the house for breakfast when Rolly drove into the yard. After the usual rural pleasantries, Rolly got down to business. "Have you got any choppers yer want ter get rid of, matey?"

Harold scratched his head. He knew it was the time of year when Rolly paid the best price for choppers but he also knew why. A few years back he had sold Rolly four older cows which hadn't got in calf, or whose milk was getting a little thin, for a better price than he could have got at the city abattoir. He'd heard later that Rolly had sold them off to some poor sod down the coast as prime in-calf milkers for twice the price he had paid Harold. So it was a matter of both conscience and pique that caused Harold to be a little suspicious of Rolly's intentions. Conscience because Rolly was likely to take somebody he knew down, and pique because he considered he'd been taken down himself in their last transaction. To solve the dilemma Harold decided whatever price Rolly offered him for this year's choppers he would up the price by ten dollars a head.

To make a long story shorter, Rolly offered Harold a very fair price for his three choppers and Harold upped the price by thirty dollars.

It was Rolly's turn to take his hat off and scratch his head. "I dunno, matey," he said. "you're makin' it a bit hard. Tell yer what I'll do though, I'll stick to me original price, but I'll throw in a real good sheep dog as well. What do yer reckon?"

"What dog?" Harold wanted to know. Rolly led Harold back to his ute and with something of a flourish swung open the passenger side door. The oldest and mangiest kelpie Harold had ever clapped eyes on dropped out at their feet. Rather than the usual rich red of a true kelpie this dog's coat was the colour and texture of a sun-dried cow pat. "There yer are, matey." Rolly said. "I call him Flash."

Harold burst out laughing. "Gawd Rolly, where'd yer get 'im from, the old dogs' home? Flash! Crikey, more like Stagger I'd say."

Rolly was a bit hurt. "Look, matey," he said, "he's a bit tired at the moment but you'd be surprised just how good this old feller can be. I've bin usin' him for the past few weeks, an' I'm not kiddin' yer when I tell yer he's the best dog I've come across for years. He treats sheep like they was his own babies. He'd be just what yer want for yer lambin' ewes next season."

Harold wasn't at all impressed. He was fully aware of Rolly's propensity to treat the truth lightly. "C'mon Rolly, I don't think the poor old bugger'll make it down to th' paddock let alone round anythin' up." He looked at Rolly a little suspiciously. "Any road, if he's as good as yer say why do yer want ter get rid of 'im?"

"Th' missus is the problem," Rolly confessed. "Old Flash is inclined to bark a bit at nights an' she reckons if I don't get rid of him she'll shoot the poor old bugger. Only last night I had to wrestle the gun out of her hands, she was so crook on his barkin'."

Harold tried not to smile at Rolly's obvious lie. The very thought of the usually meek Mrs Hills waving a loaded gun around and threatening to shoot any living thing (other than her recalcitrant husband maybe) strained the bounds of credulity. There was no way he was going to be suckered by such sob stories. "Sorry," he said. "I got two dogs now that ain't much good. I don't want another."

But Rolly wasn't beaten yet. He compromised. "Look matey," he said, "I'll tell yer what I'll do. I'll let yer set a fair trial for this dog an' if he don't make it I'll give yer the price yer askin' for them choppers an' say no more. But if he does make it then I get my price an' you keep the dog. Now I couldn't be fairer than that, could I?"

Harold considered the proposition for a few moments. He liked the idea of a bit of a gamble. Besides, one quick look in the old dog's direction showed him that it had already fallen asleep, as if the very effort of just standing for a few minutes had exhausted him. It certainly seemed a very reasonable way to make himself an extra thirty dollars. "Okay," he said eventually, "I accept."

The two of them agreed that a fair trial would be to take the dog down to the fattening paddock where Harold kept his old ewes for house meat. They agreed that if the dog could round up the sheep in five minutes or less and drive them into the killing pen they would seal the deal. Harold cast his eye on the fog beginning to come down over the home paddocks and tried to hide his smirk of triumph. If the fog got any thicker there was little chance the dog would even be able to find the ewes in a strange paddock, let alone round them up through two gates in the allotted time.

At the paddock gate Rolly took out his stop watch and put it on top of the straining post. He called Harold's attention to the time. "Okay matey," he said, "it's now five past eight. He's got till ten past. Okay?" Harold nodded his consent and Rolly concentrated his attention on the brown dog, which, during its walk down to the paddock seemed to have already developed a bit of a limp. The fog was coming in thick and fast and the dog seemed reluctant to brave it by himself. When Rolly waved the dog away and clicked his tongue loudly in the time-honoured manner, the dog just looked up at him inquiringly. With the precious seconds ticking away Rolly got impatient with the dog and gave him a quick shove with his boot in the general direction of the open gate. "Go back, yer mongrel," he growled and the dog, having finally got the message, staggered blindly off into the fog. Rolly gave Harold a bit of a sickly look. "Old Flash always was a bit slow to git goin'," he told Harold.

Harold just smirked quietly back at him as the seconds ticked by. But not for long. Quite suddenly there was the sound of a rush of hooves across the grass and the very next second nine panic-stricken ewes bounded through the paddock gate, across the lane, and into the killing pen. They hit the fence at the far side of the pen with such a thump the open gate to the pen swung closed behind them. Harold's eyes nearly fell out of his head. He hadn't counted on the possibility that as soon as the fog came down the sheep would seek shelter on the lea side of the old shed at the top end of the paddock and the dog might frighten them out rather than drive them out.

Unperturbed, Rolly consulted his watch. "One minute twenty-eight seconds exactly, by my calculations," he said. He passed the watch across to Harold who didn't even bother to look at it.

But Harold wasn't going to capitulate that easily. He considered he'd lost the bet by foul means. "That dog must have blundered into them ewes by accident," he complained. "Besides, where is he now? He's probably down there still - dropped dead from a heart attack."

Rolly dismissed Harold's plea by referring him back to their original agreement. "The deal was only that he'd get 'em in the yard, matey. It wasn't said how. Neither was it said that old Flash had ter get back in the time, or that he wouldn't cark it. A deal's a deal. Yer can't keep changin' the rules to suit yerself matey."

As they set off down the paddock to find the dog Harold prayed fervently that it had in fact died of a heart attack. He had no wish to feed and tend another useless animal. But fate was still against him. They found the dog a few minutes later, wandering aimlessly in a thick patch of thistles, completely lost. The poor old dog was so tired and bewildered Rolly had to carry him back to the house yard.

Harold could have shot the dog as soon as Rolly was gone but he wasn't a cruel man; besides, he had a lingering suspicion that Rolly had once again perpetrated a nasty trick on him and that the only way he could regain face was to get some kind of service out of the dog before its inevitable, and not too distant, end.

However, much to Harold's surprise, in the following weeks instead of the dog's condition deteriorating the opposite seemed to be happening. Good shelter and regular feeding worked wonders. The old dog began to display a new lease on life. Certainly in those first few weeks instead of a normal winter's moult, all its hair fell out, but very soon that hair was replaced by a healthy yellowish-red fluff which grew quickly and thickly all over the dog's body.

Harold couldn't believe it at first but after a more careful examination of the dog he found that in spite of the dog's teeth being black and worn it was not as old as he'd first thought. The upshot was Harold began to lavish attention on the dog. He took to feeding it night and morning, and occasionally he even added an egg or two and some cream to its meal. The dog continued to blossom. Its limp - which turned out to be nothing more than blisters on its pads - became less and less obvious and its protruding hip bones began to disappear under a nice layer of healthy flesh. Within a few weeks Harold had the dog out working the sheep.

There was no doubt he was still a bit slow but, as Rolly had said, he was as gentle as the lambs he worked. As for the continuous barking Rolly had warned about - well, that just stopped. Though whether it was because the dog had been unhappy in the past, or whether it had lost its bark from over-use, Harold couldn't tell. Maybe Rolly had lied about that too? Whatever, the fact was that after the first week in Harold's care the dog was never heard to bark again.

That red/yellow dog was Harold's almost constant companion for nearly two years before it died quietly one night in its sleep. Harold was very sad to see the dog go. So was Rolly for that matter. He ran into Harold one day about a year after he had given him the dog and watched it moving a bunch of fat lambs down the road to the railway station. The dog seemed able to anticipate every move the lambs made. He guided them through the traffic and past open gates with an almost uncanny accuracy.

Rolly was very impressed. He stopped Harold at the railway gate. "Say Harold," he said, "that sure is a real good dog yer got there. Where'd he come from?"

"Ar," Harold answered smugly, "some nong who didn't know a good dog when he saw him give him to me."

Rolly shook his head disbelievingly as he watched the dog unerringly heading the lambs towards the railway loading yards without even being told. "Well I can't understand that, matey," he said. "That dog's a winner as plain as the nose on yer face. Any time yer want to get rid of him I'll offer yer a real good price."

Harold smirked openly then. "You already have, matey," he said, and just for Rolly's benefit he gave the dog a loud whistle. "Come behind here, Flash," he shouted. "There's a good old boy."

A Taste of Pig

A distant cousin from England came to stay with Herbie Miles and his family. Herbie's cousin was a lecturer at a university in the south of England, touring Australia during his sabbatical leave. He had decided it would be interesting to look up some of those relatives on the Australian migratory tree so he could get a really good taste of the country and its people.

When Herbie picked his cousin up from the city bus and mutual introductions were completed, Herbie's cousin explained how delighted he was to be able to have the chance of staying on a real dinky-di Aussie farm. "I felt that being an ordinary tourist wasn't good enough for a chap like me," he told Herbie. "I thought a bit of a stay around with those few friends and relatives I have in this country would tell me a lot more about your ways than just travelling around in a tour bus."

"Well, how's it been then?" Herbie asked him as they drove up the road to the farm.

"So far, very illuminating," Herbie's cousin said. "And in anticipation of your next question, cousin Herbert, I find I like your country and its people very much. There is a nice balance, I think, between brash confidence and a deep-seated need to be well thought of."

"Oh," Herbie said. He wasn't quite sure whether or not his cousin was having a bit of a shot or not. But blood being thicker than water he gave his cousin the benefit of the doubt.

As they wound their way up into the hill country he gave his cousin a quick run-down on why this particular district was the best in the state, who owned what farm, what was wrong with it and how, in his opinion, it could be run better. "You wait until yer see our farm though," Herbie said. "It's the nicest little farm in the district and possibly one of the best in the state."

His cousin smiled a little. "I'll look forward to it, Herbert," he said.

At dinner that night Herbie asked his cousin whether the university he taught at was anywhere near Oxford or Cambridge. His cousin told him it wasn't, that it was much further south and Herbie, who had run out of his limited knowledge of English universities, decided then that it was safer to stick to subjects he was more familiar with. His cousin was, after all, here to learn about the Australian way of life and Herbie was quite happy to pitch in with a bit of local colour.

"How'd yer like the casserole then?" he asked.

"Absolutely first class," his cousin offered. "Top rate."

"It's pork," Herbie said. "Grown right here on this farm."

"Jolly good," his cousin said.

"Yeah," Herbie continued, "we grow the best porkers in the district. Skim milk fed. We separate our milk and send the cream to the butter factory. Some of the blokes around here send their milk to the cheese factory and then try to raise their pigs on the whey they get back. The silly sods don't seem to realise that whey is useless when it comes to raisin' pigs. It gives 'em worms yer know."

Herbie's cousin seemed quite impressed by this piece of information and so, inspired, Herbie galloped on. "Yeah, an' just to help our pigs along we feed 'em plenty of cooked turnips and chat potatoes - boiled bunnies even. None of yer soft, grain-fed pigs on this farm."

In between refusing a second helping of the casserole that Herbie's wife Florrie was offering him, the visitor managed a quick nod in Herbie's direction. "It all sounds very well organised to me, cousin Herbert," he said.

Herbie felt even more inspired by his cousin's approval and galloped on with further revelations. "Though it's a pity yer weren't here a while back. Yer could have joined in the fun."

"What is that, Herbert?"

"Pig killin' day," Herbie answered. "We killed eight of 'em just a couple of weeks back. In early May. There's no R's in May."

"Ah," his cousin said and raised his eyebrows, awaiting further information about Herbie's cryptic statement. A true blue academic, he deduced he was about to hear a genuine piece of folklore.

"We only make bacon in the months that don't have an R in 'em. When the weather's cold and settled, see? Though I must admit August can be a bit of a bugger at times."

"You make your own bacon then, Herbert?"

Herbie laughed and winked broadly at his wife and kids. "Do we? I'll say we do, an' what's more tomorrow mornin' at breakfast yer goin' to taste the nicest bit of bacon yer ever tasted."

Anyone with a greater sense of awareness than Herbie would have noticed his cousin pale slightly when he heard that piece of news. The fact was, Herbie's cousin wasn't all that fond of pork and actively detested bacon. But being the polite Englishman he was, he certainly wasn't going to say so, especially to his cousin who seemed so proud of his pork products.

After quite a nice evening, spoilt only by some "real Aussie wine" that Herbie had brought out and insisted plying his cousin with (a cask, incidentally, which Herbie and Florrie had been slowly wading through since Christmas) the cousin went off to bed claiming tiredness from travelling. But as tired as he was, he didn't sleep well. Twice during the night he got up to go to the bathroom and his hosts even thought they heard a feverish shout from his bedroom in the early hours of the morning. "Probably due to all that travelling and another strange bed," Florrie suggested to Herbie when they heard the footsteps in the hall for the second time.

But, whatever it was, there seemed no signs of any discomfort the following morning. Their visitor not only rose early to watch Herbie and Florrie do the milking, he even managed to get a short walk up the road and back before breakfast. Quite a heavy breakfast as it turned out, consisting of porridge and clotted cream, fried eggs with sliced kidneys and several rashers of the fatty bacon Herbie had promised the night before.

The cousin nodded bravely as he nibbled his way through the bulky fare. "First class, cousin Florrie," he said. "Top notch."

Although, as Herbie observed later, his cousin didn't seem quite as fond of the fat as he was of the lean. He cut most of the fat off and Florrie later fed it to the house cat. Herbie assumed it was most likely an English habit not to eat bacon fat.

*"It's all part of the pig ...
We don't waste anythin'..."*

Their long-suffering visitor offered the same praise at midday lunch after he and Herbie came back from looking over the top paddocks of the farm and Florrie had dished up some thickly buttered bread and cold pork brawn. And then again that evening when, after doing little but listen to the many and varied schemes Herbie had for the improvement of the farm in the future, they sat down to generous platefuls of pork spare ribs and baked potatoes.

"It's all part of the pig," Herbie told his cousin proudly as he stabbed at one of the ribs with his fork. "We don't waste anythin'- not one little scrap. It all gets used one way or another."

By that time Herbie's cousin didn't seem particularly impressed, for even though he kept up an incessant smiling and nodding of appreciation as he gnawed his way through rib after rib, his smiles were becoming somewhat strained.

"My word," he said eventually as he pushed his half-eaten plate of ribs away and patted his stomach. "My word ... all this food. I really must watch my waist-line."

"That's probably why he left some of 'em," Florrie suggested to Herbie when they had gone to bed.

Herbie agreed. "Yeah, I reckon yer right, Florrie, but don't worry, tommorra I'll give him a bit more exercise. I'll take him right down to the bottom paddocks an' show him what a real nice bunch of dairy heifers look like."

So, the following morning, after another heavy breakfast of bacon, eggs and pork sausages, Herbie and his visitor set out for the bottom paddocks. As they walked down the track Herbie continued to hold forth with his esoteric knowledge of farming in a moderate climate and its relative attributes. "We got it all over those poor buggers on the mainland," he explained to his cousin as they made their way through the lush green paddocks. "We can grow white clover here like yer wouldn't believe, an' rye grass thicker than the hairs on a wombat's back."

Herbie had taken the wire strainers with him in case any of the fences needed tightening and sure enough they found one that had been badly mauled by the mob of dairy heifers trying to get into a paddock of autumn oats and rye grass. "Little blighters," Herbie growled without any note of real rancour when they found the fence. "I'll send 'em off to the abatto'rs if they do it again."

Herbie's cousin was a little shocked. "Would you really do that, Herbert?" he asked.

"Good God no," Herbie said from behind his hand. "They're worth too much t' sell. I'm just givin' them a bit of a fright." He passed his cousin the hammer and staples. "Here yer go," he said, "you can nail the wire up if yer like. You'll be able to tell 'em back home yer worked on a dinky-di Aussie farm." Herbie winked at his cousin then and offered him another bit of homespun philosophy. "There's nothin' like a bit of outdoor work ter build up the appetite, don't yer reckon?"

"It is indeed a rare chance," Herbie's cousin said as he took the staples and hammer.

Herbie recounted his experience with his English cousin a few days later in the pub. Apparently his cousin had not seemed too familiar with a hammer. Herbie reckoned his cousin bent more staples than went into the fence.

"He just couldn't seem to get th' gist of it at all. Like he couldn't hold them proper. An' talk about green - that's what colour he went after he'd been at it a while. It didn't seem he could cope with all that bendin'."

According to Herbie he became a little concerned when his cousin pleaded a halt. His cousin was his responsibility after all. "You don't seem too sprightly," he observed anxiously.

"Oh, it's nothing really," his cousin answered without conviction. "Just a bit of a headache and a heck of a thirst."

"Ah," Herbie said, "I reckon it was them pork sausages of Florrie's. I told her she put too much salt in 'em."

He took his cousin across to a nearby water trough and held the ball tap open. "Here," he said, "get some water inter yer - it's not real good water but it's clean enough."

Herbie's cousin bent over the trough and took several long gulps of the water. But instead of improving things it had the opposite effect. His cousin suddenly seemed in danger of choking to death. Herbie watched amazed as he saw his cousin draw back from the trough and spit out the water he hadn't swallowed. His visitor's face wasn't green any longer. It was deathly white. "My God it tastes awful," he groaned with considerable anguish.

"Well," Herbie answered a little petulantly, "I did warn yer it wasn't the best - it's bore water, yer see."

At that point Herbie's English cousin was suddenly and violently sick in the trough and all over Herbie's boots as well...

It may have simply been an association of ideas that had made Herbie's cousin sick like that - a vague memory perhaps that none of the pig was ever wasted - not one little scrap! But in truth it was more likely due to the fact his stomach had been constantly assaulted with fatty, salty pork since his arrival at the Miles' farm. Especially in view of the fact he had never much liked pork and actively detested bacon. Still, Herbie didn't know that, and whenever he told the story later he always insisted on giving the former interpretation.

"I know he's an educated man an' all," he said, as a way of summing up the unfortunate episode, "but then when it comes to education I always reckon too much of it can sometimes be worse than none at all. Yer know what I mean? Yer brains can sometimes run away with yer common sense."

The Devils, the Butcher, and the Rotary Barbecue

Ron Saw owned one of the two butcher shops in the district. Ron had never had much schooling but he was as sharp as a prickle when it came to a bit of the old repartee. He was a very communicative man in early middle-age who seemed to enjoy working at his trade. If you'd asked him he probably would have told you that he was happy with his lot. In fact the only thing that really taxed his good nature were the few farmers in the district who killed their own stock and then "back-doored" the meat to friends and relatives at wholesale rates.

Because of this constant source of annoyance Ron was often forced into an uneasy alliance with Russ Chalmers, the local veterinarian and Council Health Inspector. In Ron's eyes Russ was a busy-body always sticking his nose in where it wasn't wanted. But in spite of that Ron also admitted Russ was a necessary watchdog when it came to catching some of those cheeky buggers whose illegal meat-selling was depriving hard-working butchers like himself out of their legitimate incomes.

It wasn't that Ron himself had anything much to fear from Russ Chalmers poking about from time to time - his shop was as clean and well run as any country butcher shop in the State - it was just that Russ Chalmers was the sort of man whose supercilious attitude implied more than he actually said. Even when Russ came into the shop as a customer his eyes were never still; he was forever peering past you with a fixed frown of disapproval, in Ron's mind trying to catch him out with a dirty chopping block perhaps, or a dead blow fly. And when Russ walked out clutching his parcel of meat Ron was never quite sure what the man's parting sniff implied. Because of that sniff Ron always trod very delicately when Russ Chalmers was within sight, or earshot.

Ron's assistant was his cousin George Saw. Unlike Ron, George wasn't at all sharp. In fact it could be said that George was as thick as the proverbial two planks. But when it came to killing and skinning animals nobody in the District could do it better than George Saw. In his own way George was a craftsman who took a craftsman's pride in a job well done. And, curiously enough, contrary to what some might think, George was also a very emotional man who was often known to wax eloquent over the carcasses of the animals he had slaughtered the previous day. Pig carcasses especially seemed to move his soul.

"Ain't they lovely?" he'd say to visitors who came to his shed for any reason. He would run his big square hands lightly up and down the sides of the unblemished white skin as delicately and seductively as a lover. Then, as if to create his own accolade, he'd give the smooth solid carcass a mighty slap that would reverberate around the concrete killing shed. "Solid as a rock," he'd say with great satisfaction. "Solid as a bloody rock." The script was always the same.

Because of the health regulations the killing shed had been built well out of town. On Sundays and Mondays George would be out at the shed slaughtering and dressing the two beasts, fourteen or so sheep and five pigs that were needed to stock the shop each week. On those days he started at seven in the morning and more often than not worked right through until dark. On one such pig-killing day George was having trouble keeping up the supply of scalding water. It had been a particularly wet spring in the district and the wood he was using to fire the boiler was damp and a bit rotten. It was well after dark when he finished and in his hurry to get home to his nice hot dinner George forgot to double check that the steel plates at the bottom of the slaughter-house door were firmly in place.

When he returned in the morning to collect the five pig carcasses he was somewhat shocked by the sight of the steel plates pushed to one side and the bottom of the wire door torn to shreds. Suspecting someone had been pilfering the pork overnight, he rushed into the shed where he was greeted by the most amazing sight. The pig carcasses were still hanging where he'd left them the night before, but now only the back legs and a few inches of brisket remained. What was left of the heads and larger bones lay scattered from one end of the killing shed floor to the other. The whole place looked more like a desecrated graveyard than an abattoir.

George was devastated. "Them bastards..." he yelled, and with such force it was surprising his cry of agony and remorse wasn't heard in the distant township. Ten minutes later, white-faced and still shaking, he staggered into Ron's butcher's shop and repeated his wrathful shout.

Ron sat him down on the meat block and tried to calm him. "What are you talkin' about George. Who's a bastard?" George began waving his arms around like he was being attacked by a savage swarm of killer bees. "Them bastards what ate me pigs."

Ron was beginning to lose his patience. "What the hell are you talking about George? Just give it to me straight, ay."

"Devils," George moaned in the most abject manner. "Them little four-legged spotty bastards. They chopped 'em off ... clean as a whistle." Saying it out loud had the effect of reminding him again of the terrible sight of the half-eaten pig carcasses. He rolled his head as if in terrible pain. Great tears welled up in his eyes and rolled down his ruddy cheeks.

It was Ron's turn to chuck a wobbly when he finally understood what George was on about. He grabbed George by his coat and shook him violently. "Are you tryin' to tell me, George, that you let a pack of devils eat our bloody pigs?"

Of course George realised it was due to his own carelessness that the accident had happened in the first place but he wasn't about to take all the blame himself. "It's them plates," he said, "they never did fit proper."

But Ron wasn't in the mood for such trivial excuses. He was dumbstruck by the consequences of such a catastrophe. His pork orders each week were a considerable part of his income, not to mention, that was, any disappointment his pork-loving clientele might endure when faced with the possibility of a porkless week. In his mind's eye he envisaged the looks of blank outrage he would receive when he had to explain what had happened to their orders ... they would go to his rival on the other side of the town to get their chump chops and spare ribs. That's what they'd do. And who was to say they wouldn't keep going there!

Outraged by his visions of bankruptcy and ruin he grabbed hold of George's collar and shook him again. "Are you sure they got at all the carcasses George?"

"Sure I'm sure," George shouted. "They ate their way through the wire an' chomped 'em off right up to their middle ribs."

With those words Ron thought he saw a glimmer of hope. He let go of George's collar and his voice took on a more conciliatory tone. "Middle ribs you said, George; so you'd say they was half eaten rather than full eaten?"

"What's the difference?" George wanted to know, "they're all ruined anyway."

"Now, hang on a second..." Ron held his hand out flat, parallel to the floor. He began moving it up and down a bit. There was a kind of cold calculating expression on his face. "I mean, George, even standin' on its back legs a full grown devil couldn't reach more than say three feet or so, could it?"

Ron made a quick decision then. He instructed George to go back to the killing shed and retrieve the damaged carcasses. "So's I can see how bad it is. You never know what we might be able to do, ay." He made it sound all very casual. It was only the sense of urgency in his final instruction to George that gave him away. "An' George, whatever you do you don't let anyone other than me see 'em, okay."

George wasn't quite sure what Ron was on about, but Ron was the boss, and in the circumstances it seemed best to humour him. Without another word he scooted off in the van and before thirty minutes was up he was back with the remains of the pig carcasses tightly wrapped in their white sheets. Ron hustled him into the cool-room and immediately began removing the sheets. When he saw what the devils had done he couldn't help giving a short whistle of admiration. "Strewth, neat as you like. The little buggers must have teeth like razors."

George wasn't so impressed. "It's a wonder they got any teeth left after tearin' that bloody great hole in me wire door."

Ron didn't bother to listen to his cousin's moaning, he was still thoughtfully contemplating the five half-eaten carcasses. There wasn't a mark or blemish beyond the ragged rib-line. He looked hastily out through the cool-room door. "Keep your eye open for any early customers, George," he said, and without further word he whipped out his trimming knife and set about taking a few inches off each of the carcasses.

George watched him at first with some puzzlement, then, when he finally realised what his cousin was up to, his initial puzzlement was replaced by an expression of horror. "Strewth Ron, you ain't goin' to sell 'em out, are yer?"

Ron didn't bother to answer immediately, he merely motioned impatiently for George to pick up the frayed bits and pieces and put them into the waste bag. It was only when he had finished trimming up the last pig that he gave his attention to George's question. "Have you got a better idea, George? I paid a lot for them pigs, an' I'm not givin' 'em over to the dogs without a try. Anyway, nobody's goin' to be hurt, an' nobody's goin' to know if you keep your big trap closed. Now, how about you goin' back to the shed an' cleanin' up. An' this time don't forget to fix those bloody plates when you leave."

George was still hesitant. "But crikey Ron, what if Russ finds out - you could lose yer licence."

"Yeah," Ron answered, "an' if I listened to you I could throw out the rest of this perfectly good pork an' charge the whole bloody lot against your wages."

George might have been a bit dim but he got Ron's meaning well enough. He was out the back door of the shop and into the meat van before Ron had the half carcasses back on their respective hooks...

As it turned out Ron found it wasn't an easy job selling off the remainder of the pork in spite of the fact it was only half of his weekly quota. On average, two out of every three customers who wanted pork that week wanted the cheaper neck or shoulder chops. Nobody seemed interested in buying hind legs at all. Only a quick wit and a smooth tongue, tempered by desperation, saw the first two days out.

"Sorry, Mrs Booth, sold right out of pork shoulder this week - still I'll tell you what I'll do, seein' you're one of my favourite customers - I'll give you a nice piece of rump for the same price. Now I couldn't be fairer than that, could I?"

Ron calculated that what he would lose on the expensive cuts he would gain in goodwill and, of course, divert the possibility of anyone becoming curious as to why there were no cheap cuts of pork left so early in the week. He also realised that as each day went by the problem would lessen. Come Thursday morning he was even beginning to smile again. That was until Russ Chalmers walked into the shop.

Ron's lingering guilty conscience immediately jumped to the fore. Perhaps George had blabbed the story about the pigs in the pub? The very thought of it had the effect of turning Ron's legs to water. The slam of the shop door behind Russ sounded strangely metallic and foreboding. His usual easy patter deserted him and instead of keeping his cool he began to babble like an idiot. "Good afternoon ... eh, I should say morning, Russ ... eh, Mr Chalmers, what can I do for you? Come to get a nice piece of beef I suppose ... the best I've had for several weeks I might say."

Russ Chalmers looked at Ron curiously. Up till now it had always been Russ this and Russ that, and now suddenly...? Being a naturally suspicious man he knew immediately that Ron was up to something. He gave a swift glance around the shop. There certainly seemed to be nothing amiss. The shop was as clean and tidy as he expected it to be. Perhaps, he thought, Ron was sickening for something. He certainly looked a little flushed in the face.

"No thanks, Ron, just the shoulder of pork my wife ordered last week." Ron's patter dried up suddenly when he realised that in his panic he had forgotten to check through the late week orders. And, to prove the axiom that panic makes a bad liar, he immediately resorted to bluster. "Oh..." he said. "No ... I think there's been a bit of a mistake Russ ... eh ... if I remember correctly Mrs Chalmers ordered a mutton rib-roast." He began to feign a quick search through his order book, stabbing at random with his extended finger amongst his written orders. "Yes, I was right Russ, she did, a rib-roast ... got it down right here."

Russ Chalmers was not impressed by Ron's little ploy. "We hate mutton, you should know that, Ron." He leant across the counter, reaching for the order book. "Here give me a look."

Ron slammed the book closed and prayed the floor would open up and swallow him. But of course it didn't so he just stood there, his face making out like a traffic light. He'd been caught out well and truly and there seemed only one action left to him. He turned quickly and almost ran into the cool-room. A few seconds later he reappeared carrying a whole hind leg of pork which he dropped onto the chopping block. "I'm sorry," he told Russ, "I must have got it wrong. Look Russ ... as a token of goodwill ... I'll let you have this leg of pork for the same price as the shoulder. Now I couldn't be fairer than that, could I?"

Russ Chalmers couldn't believe his luck. Even though he was sure that Ron was up to something he had no idea what it might be. He was trying to work out what kind of misdemeanour was worth the difference between a piece of pork brisket and a very generous hind leg. Not a lot, he thought finally, so he agreed to the offer before Ron changed his mind. He took the leg of pork and prepared to depart, but not before he had taken his usual quick look around the shop and given Ron his very best supercilious sniff. As he walked back to his car he vowed to himself he would keep a much closer eye on Ron in the future.

Ron didn't get a lot of sleep that night. His wife complained the following morning at breakfast that he had kept her awake with his tossing and turning. "At one time," she told him, "you even sat up with your arms beatin' around your head like you was tryin' to fly or somethin' ... or beat something off. You were shoutin' if I remember correct ... somethin' about flyin' pigs an' barbecues."

She was then quite horrified to see her husband's reaction to this latest piece of information. He literally threw his half-eaten toast down on to the table and galloped from the room shouting, "My God, the pig roast..."

Poor Ron. In the turmoil of that week he had forgotten he was supposed to save a whole pig for the Rotary Club's annual fund raising spectacular. Talking a few customers out of the front end of a porker was one thing; there was no way he was going to talk the Rotarians into spit roasting half of a pig! Back in his shop he paced up and down behind the counter trying to think what he could do. He imagined the looming confrontation between himself and the club's president, Colonel Foote - he on one side of the counter and the Colonel on the other -

leaning forward, red-faced and furious, demanding to know where the Rotarians were going to stick an apple in a headless pig.

"Ring Morrie down the coast," George suggested when he returned from his Friday deliveries. Ron scowled at him. "D'you think I haven't already thought of that, George. I've rung every butcher from here to the city an' nobody's got a scrap of pork to spare at this time of the week."

George could easily see that Ron wasn't in the mood for any chitchat so he decided it would be best if he just did his jobs and let Ron work it out for himself. It had all become too much for George's simple mind. All he wanted was to return to those uncomplicated pre-devil days when his cousin was an easy-going friend rather than a miserable tyrant.

It was young Tom, Rolly Hills' new assistant, who eventually saved the day. He had come in to the shop to buy a piece of pork for Mrs Hills, though Ron didn't appreciate that at the time. In his renewed state of paranoia he was still too busy contemplating the possibility that Russ Chalmers might have taken the leg of pork as evidence - that at this very moment he had it under the microscope back at the council chambers. Or that the phone would ring and it would be the secretary of the Rotary Club demanding his roasting pig. Consequently, when Ron heard the word pork, he almost shouted at young Tom. He imagined in his vulnerable state of mind that his long-time enemy Rolly Hills might have even sent his young assistant into the shop just to rile him.

"I suppose you want a shoulder, or a head to turn into brawn, or the front trotters maybe, for some special pagan rite. Well, you can tell your boss I've got better things to do than mess about with practical jokes."

Young Tom drew himself up to his full five feet three inches and challenged Ron's strange behaviour with a confidence born from being the new offsider to the smartest operator in the district. "As a matter of fact, Mr Saw," he said in his most haughty Cockney-Australian accent, "I wanted a piece of pork 'ind leg what's not too fatty fer Mrs 'ills ter roast fer next Sundy; but seein' yer in such a lousy mood I'll git some darn th' coast later this arvo."

As young Tom turned to walk out Ron suddenly saw the light of understanding. He literally galloped around the corner of the counter to block the exit. As he faced Tom, his expression - his whole, bowed frame - was one of abject contrition; one could even say, of supplication. The tone of his voice was more than conciliatory. It was downright pleading. "Look Tom, I'm sorry, I don't know what got into me. I haven't been myself lately. I think I'm coming down with the flu. Don't take any notice of what I said, ay."

Once he had made sure Tom wasn't leaving, he raced back to the cool room and got out the last half carcass. As he was preparing it, he

How come his traditional antagonist was suddenly so desperate for a porker?

continued to explain to Tom about his troubles. "I've had a bad week all around with my orders, Tom. Everyone wants what I haven't got an' it's gettin' to me." He shoved the parcel across the counter and forced himself to give young Tom what he hoped was a man-of-the-world to another man-of-the-world smile. "Look Tom, you get around a bit, d'you know anyone who might have a nice porker? I could do with some extra pork this week."

"Sure I do," young Tom told him. "Rolly's got one." Ron gulped and his countenance turned from amber to red again. He had another problem now. Rolly was after all the king of the "back-doorers" and sworn enemy. If he took a pig from Rolly it would not only seem like he was condoning all of Rolly's past misdemeanours but his future ones as well. But then - as they say - desperation is as desperation does. "I'll take him," Ron declared with some finality. Tell Rolly I'll take him..." He almost caught himself out by adding "at any price" but stopped himself just in time.

"Righty-oh," young Tom answered with a puzzled cheeriness. And, taking advantage of Ron's distracted state of mind, he left the shop without paying for his piece of pork leg.

Rolly was also puzzled when Tom passed the message on. How come his traditional antagonist was suddenly so desperate for a porker? Being the kind of pragmatist who couldn't help contemplating gain from other's misfortunes Rolly thought there might be more in the deal than the casual quid pro quo. He decided it would be an interesting exercise to try to extract as much as he could out of the unlikely situation. He waited long enough to give Ron a real dose of the heeby-jeebies before he fronted up at Ron's shop later that afternoon.

Ron tried his best to greet Rolly amicably and casually. He tried the first couple of lines from his well rehearsed mental script. "Ah, Rolly," he said. "I thought you might like me to take that porker of yours off yer hands. I need a bit of extra pork for the weekend. If he's any good, that is."

But Ron's accompanying smile of greeting didn't fool Rolly one little bit. The butcher's smile, Rolly thought gleefully, was more the fixed nervous smile of a reluctant debutante than the casual, mutual interest smile of a prospective buyer. There was no way that someone like Rolly, who had spent a lifetime of reading other's faces, was going to be suckered by that phony smirk. He realised immediately that it was a sellers' market.

"He's a good un alright Ron. As a matter of fact growin' so well I'd almost decided ter take him on ter bacon. I mean, what with young Tom spotting that heap of cheap grain last month, I got plenty of feed an' all. Depends on the price I suppose."

The lines Ron had rehearsed so many times while he was waiting for Rolly to show disintegrated into a series of ehs and ums before Rolly's simple ultimatum. His shoulders visibly slumped. Time was running out. What was the point of arguing? "Okay, okay, Rolly, I'll take him," was all he said.

Rolly, of course, hit up the price, and a very subdued Ron Saw agreed that Rolly would drop the porker off at the killing shed within the hour. Rolly left Ron's shop that afternoon with the same vague puzzlement that Russ Chalmers had experienced earlier. Not only had Ron Saw broken his oft-stated pledge never to buy anything from Rolly, he had paid him a better price for the porker than he could have got anywhere else. Naturally enough Rolly also vowed he would keep a closer eye on Ron Saw in the future. The butcher was up to something and Rolly felt that if he could find out just what that something was it could be very beneficial, one way or another.

The full irony of the fiasco, however, wasn't revealed until later that night when the secretary of the Rotary Club rang Ron at home and told him that owing to unforeseen circumstances the Rotary barbecue was off. "It's the Colonel," the secretary said apologetically, "he's had another bad turn, an' as you know, Ron, the fund raisin' pig roast tomorrow night was goin' to be down at his place ... the rest of us office bearers thought it would be diplomatic to put it off for a couple of weeks. I mean, the noise - an' him sick in bed an' all."

"Christ!" Ron shouted down the phone. "Couldn't you lot hold the bloody barbie somewhere else?"

The secretary was sympathetic. "Yeah, I take your point Ron, but you know the Colonel, he's a bit touchy about things like that."

Ron knew the Colonel alright. In his opinion he was only in Rotary to get an MBE anyway. "Bugger the Colonel, and bugger the pig as well," Ron shouted down the phone.

The secretary was a little worried about Ron's uncharacteristic display of temperament. He decided a little appeasement might be in order. "I suppose we could still take the pig an' flog him around to our members," he suggested. It was the worst thing he could have said. The phone crashed in his ear.

Not surprisingly, Ron's strange behaviour that week was the talk of the district for some time after. Why had such an amiable bloke turned into a sourpuss overnight? It was one of those small mysteries that intrigued the locals. Some suggested it may have been his thyroid running amok; others that his wife was having an affair with the new lines foreman who had been a constant visitor to the Saws' house around that time; and others again that it was something to do with mid-life crises.

In spite of his constant endeavours, Rolly Hills never got anywhere near finding out the true explanation for Ron's strange behaviour that week. And it could be said that even though Russ Chalmers didn't find out either, he did hear the truth the following week. It just didn't register at the time.

Russ had run into George Saw in the local pub and offered to shout him a beer. Even someone of George's limited mental ability could work out what all that was about. He could see no way out, he just nodded dumbly and waited for Russ' inevitable question.

"Tell me George," Russ said when he'd taken his first sip of beer, "has Ron really gone mad or is he up to something shady?"

George pulled several amazing faces as he grappled with the seeming unanswerable question. If he answered at all it was inevitable he would dob in his boss one way or another. In the end he did the only thing possible. He slapped his untouched beer back down on the bar and ran out of the pub.

Russ looked after him with astonishment before he turned his attention back to Pat the barman. "It's my personal opinion the pair of them have flipped," he said. "What do you reckon Pat?"

Pat gave him a faint apologetic smile as he polished the glass in his hand. He had learnt long ago how dangerous it was to engage in idle bar-room gossip. "Ah, th' Devil only knows, Russ," he answered.

Christmas Goose

In the late autumn Herbie Miles bought a gander and two geese at a local sale for the price of two dollars. When he got back to his farm that evening he insisted that his wife Florrie come and check the bargain out. Packed together in an old wire cage, flight feathers bedraggled and broken, they looked to Florrie a very woebegone threesome. She wasn't at all impressed and didn't hesitate to say so.

"Don't worry old girl," Herbie said with his usual optimism. "They're a bit old an' a bit rough but they'll fatten up real nice by Christmas, you wait an' see. It'll complement that nice bit of ham we saved. An' it'll be a darn sight cheaper, too, than havin' to kill off another fat lamb ter feed those hungry relatives of yours who turn up every Christmas."

Florrie Miles' only response was a slight sniff. She had learnt long ago to expect very little from Herbie when it came to forward planning. It was said in the district that the only reason she put up with her husband was because she was a natural nurturer and couldn't help herself. It was rare that she didn't have some small stray creature bleating or meowing at her heels. Herbie, it was said, was just another of those unfortunate creatures she was bound by her instincts to nurture, no matter what.

And as far as the other farmers in the District were concerned the only reason they put up with Herbie was because he was a trier and a worker. It was a reputation Herbie accepted as his rightful due, seeing his favourite saying was: "If everybody in this country worked as hard as I do, Australia ud be the richest country in the world."

But then, as far as Herbie was concerned, hard work wasn't the way to riches after all. There was a flaw in his reasoning. His closest neighbour Ossie Nichols explained it one night at a farmers' meeting. He suggested the reason Herbie didn't have time to attend meetings was he was too busy digging himself another hole to jump in. "Remember the time he was goin' to make a killin' on pigeon peas? He got so enthusiastic about it all that he jus' kept on ploughin' his paddock all night. By the time the sun come up next mornin' you'd have sworn a whole tribe of wild pigs had been at it. So what does old Herbie do? He spends all the next day straightenin' it out. Herbie's methods just don't make sense. It's a kind of one step forward two steps back sort of thing."

However, Herbie wasn't the kind of bloke to be put off by others' opinions, especially if the opinion came from his wife Florrie who always seemed to take great delight in pouring cold water on his ideas. When she turned up her nose and walked away the day he bought the geese, he became even more determined to prove her wrong. He calculated that even if the very worst thing happened and all three of the geese kicked the bucket he'd only lose two miserable dollars. He only had to fatten one of them and he'd be well in front. How could such a simple calculation as that go wrong?

But, as often seemed to happen in Herbie's case, go wrong it did. Herbie hadn't considered all possible contingencies. But that's not saying the geese didn't do well right from the start. According to the story the geese thrived on their new fare of clover and rye grass. It was old Maisie, the Miles' winter milker, that was the problem. The usually placid old cow had begun to show uncharacteristic signs of irritation ever since Herbie had turned the three noisy geese loose in her paddock. By the end of the first week her milk output had plummeted.

The Miles' thirteen year old son was the first one to call a warning. It was Clarie's job to milk the cow before and after school. He told his old man that the geese were not only taking the best pick of clover away from Maisie, they were also fouling what they didn't eat with their droppings and it wasn't surprising that old Maisie objected.

"She'll get used to 'em in a few days," Herbie told his son with his usual confidence. But after the cow had kicked her bucket over two mornings in succession even Herbie had to accept there was a problem. He reluctantly agreed to do something about it.

"I'll just have to find 'em another paddock," he conceded that evening at dinner.

Clarie was glad to hear it, and so was Florrie for that matter. She also had been constantly complaining about the geese. "Just make sure it's a long way away, Herbert," she told her husband, "preferably on someone else's property. It's their yabberin' an' screechin' that I can't abide. If they keep me awake just one more night I'll take the axe to 'em meself, I swear."

Herbie was a bit upset by what he thought was unfair comment, but he was also wise enough to know that his wife rarely made idle threats and that, in spite of her nurturing instincts, geese did not seem to be on her list of protected species. He was, after all, only trying to save money by buying the geese.

"Don't you worry," he told Florrie. "I'll take 'em away. But, by golly, when I bring them back all nice and fat for Christmas I'll expect you ter eat yer words as well as the geese."

He decided to move the geese in with his breeding ewes. Sheep weren't nearly as particular as Jersey house cows. They wouldn't mind three ring-ins for a few weeks, he thought. But once again Herbie's optimism was short-lived, for although the geese continued to thrive, the ewes, which had only recently finished lambing, didn't. The simple fact was the gander, which was sensible enough to have avoided any confrontation with the house cow, Maisie, seemed to consider these lesser creatures were to be despised. If any sheep or lamb dared come too close to either of his two mates he was inclined to charge at them with flapping wings and hissing, outstretched beak. More than once Herbie had to spend precious time re-mothering stray lambs which had become lost in the ensuing battle between ewe and gander. It was becoming imperative he move the geese again.

This time he chose the long hill-paddock which was more exposed but which the geese would have all to themselves for the entire winter period. "They'll be okay there right up until Christmas," he said to his wife. "You'll be surprised how they look next time you see 'em."

The only problem was the geese were now so far away that Herbie had very little time to see them himself. When he did finally get around to it in the late spring he was more than a little miffed to find that the geese had somewhat over-thrived in the meantime. They had managed to hatch out sixteen tiny goslings between them.

"I can't kill any of 'em for this Christmas," he grumbled to his family that night. "The young 'uns will die without their parents' protection."

So, instead of the fat geese he had promised, Herbie was once more obliged to kill one of his prime fat lambs to feed the inevitable army of relatives who turned up for the Christmas feast. And it should be said none of them were heard to grumble about the non-traditional fare. Except Herbie, of course, who spoilt his own dinner by thinking goose rather than lamb. He could only compensate for his disappointment with the thought that next Christmas things would be different. Next Christmas there would not only be geese aplenty to feed all those relatives, there would also be enough left over to sell and boost their income.

The hill paddock he'd moved the geese to was the largest and steepest on the farm. Although the top third was reasonably flat, it soon fell away through clumps of ferns, bedfordia bushes, and fireweed to a dank, wet gully. It was certainly too steep and dangerous to plough, a fact that was a constant source of annoyance to Herbie because its soil was very fertile and would have grown any crop you like, had he been able to buy or hire a cat tractor, and if the crop could ever have been harvested, which it couldn't. Consequently it was the kind of paddock Herbie used only for fattening animals which he had culled from his herd at the end of the season. He decided the geese might just as well stay there until Christmas next.

Herbie rarely caught sight of the geese for weeks at a time, though once, in passing, he witnessed the gander engaged in a very one-sided battle with a young wedge-tailed eagle which had foolishly thought one of the half-grown goslings would make an easy prey. From a short distance away Herbie watched the swift dive with horror. He was sure the eagle would get one of the half-grown goslings. He ripped his old hat off and threw it upwards towards the swooping eagle, hoping it would distract the bird's attention, but it was too late - way too late. The eagle was already levelling out its dive, talons extended ready for the kill.

That was the moment the gander chose its time to retaliate. Neck extended, wings thrashing, it moved swiftly into the eagle's flight path. Instead of the nice fat gosling the eagle expected, it was more of a honking, hissing, fire-eating dragon it was heading directly for now. It was all too much for the eagle. It lost its nerve. Its tail feathers fanned out in a last-second bid to change direction, causing its initial predatory swoop to become no more than an inglorious, poorly-executed, crash-landing into a clump of scrub at the paddock's edge. It was a much humbled bird that emerged, feathers askew, and flapped off towards the safety of the high trees on the far hill.

Thus assured that the flock of geese could only but thrive under such a fierce protector, Herbie left them to get on with their growing and fattening.

It was only when he heard their distant honking clamour on windless nights that he gave the geese any thought at all. Until, that was, the Christmas season came around again and Herbie set out for the fattening paddock with his best sheep dog. He had already decided to kill and dress two of the geese for his own table. The rest he would either sell to the local butcher or keep as breeders for the following year.

As he expected, the flock was quietly grazing their way through the most sheltered and lush corner of the large steep paddock. Also as he expected, the moment the gander spotted him with dog at heel it went into its outstretched head-and-wings battle mode. Not that it worried Herbie. During the eighteen months' residency of the geese on his farm he had managed to pick up a few points on the art of goose farming. With the aid of a long stick and a bit of nifty sidestepping that would have done credit to an experienced matador, he managed to deflect the gander's constant barrage of wings and beak with consummate ease. Then, by using his dog as a decoy, he managed to cut the rest of the flock off from their most obvious retreat down-hill.

But the gander was an old hand, too. Immediately he realised his flock was being divided, he changed his tactics. Instead of doing battle with Herbie's stick and dog, he made one quick dash right through

Herbie's open legs. Wings outstretched, and in high honking triumph, he set off down the hill with the remainder of the flock in tow.

Equally as determined, Herbie and the dog galloped after them and it wasn't until they were half way down the hill that Herbie realised the danger. The fact was the gander was moving so fast into the wind its feet were already losing contact with the ground. It took only a small wind shift from the north and the gander was suddenly and completely airborne.

Herbie could only watch in fascinated horror as the entire flock followed the gander's lead. En masse they rose up and over the gully, cawing and screeching at their unexpected dilemma. Heads and feet waggling from side to side they lifted higher and higher and grew smaller and smaller as they were caught on each new updraught of wind from the gully until the entire flock eventually shrank to mere dots and then disappeared altogether into the hazy dish of the morning sky. Heading, Herbie calculated miserably, in the general direction of the south island of New Zealand. No-one in the district, or along the coast, ever reported seeing any of them again.

To keep his promise to himself, as much to his wife and her relatives, Herbie felt obliged that Christmas to buy a couple of dressed geese from Saw's butchery. It cost him money enough, but that was nothing to what it cost him in lost pride. Nevertheless Herbie was a stickler for justice right to the end. As he glared around the table at Florrie's relatives tearing into his profit margins, Herbie Miles, ex-goose-farmer, was busy making another plan for the future. Next Christmas, he thought nastily, I'll come out on top for a change. I'll turn it into a commercial proposition. I'll charge the flamin' lot of 'em board an' bloody lodgin's.

The Much Travelled Boar

In a weak moment Ossie Nichols had once let Rolly Hills do him a small favour. Ossie, everyone said, should have known better because it was a known fact that, as far as Rolly was concerned, a favour given was a negotiable commodity.

Rolly made that point himself one day when he had Ossie trapped in the corner of the township hardware store. Which was bad enough, but add that to the fact the store was a great echoing barn of a place where even the quietest and most confidential secrets had a habit of getting picked up by a well-trained and alert ear, and you've got the idea.

Rolly's voice echoed through the store, "Ar, c'mon matey, jus' a small favour. In return for the one I did you last month ... remember? Went out of my way, I reckon - to pick up them electric fence posts for yer. But I din' mind. I mean what are friends for, I always say. So what do yer reckon?"

Outside in the open spaces Ossie could have handled such blatant coercion by reminding Rolly of all the favours, voluntary and otherwise, he had done for him over the years. But after a quick squint around the store, in which he ascertained at least three shop assistants and half a dozen customers were also hanging out for his reply, he realised he had to be a wee bit careful with his answer. He didn't want it getting around he was mean-minded. He gulped slightly and lowered his voice to reply, hoping that Rolly might do the same. "Perhaps? What do yer want Rolly?"

Rolly knew he had the upper hand and wasn't going to be sucked in by Ossie's feeble attempts to conduct the conversation in private. His voice continued to boom out through the shop. "I just want yer to look after an animal for me for a day or two, that's all."

Out of the corner of his eye Ossie noted some of the interested listeners giving brief nods of their personal sanction to such a reasonable request. He considered in the circumstances he had little choice but to also nod his approval. But his experience with Rolly told him also to temper his nod with a further hasty question. "What kind of animal, Rolly?"

"A beautiful large white pedigree boar, old matey. Quiet as a little lamb."

Ossie groaned inwardly. He'd looked after a Jersey bull for Rolly once which, having gutsed itself to its eyeballs on his best clover, had taken it into its head to move on to the next farm - through five post and rail gates. The only compensation he got for that was the firewood from the shattered rails.

He took another quick peek around the shop to see how the interested on-lookers were taking this further bit of information. This time he ascertained it was roughly a fifty-fifty split of opinion. On the strength of that, he gave his somewhat equivocal answer. "I'll give it some thought Rolly," he said. And before Rolly could come up with some further diabolical plan of attack, Ossie fled the shop.

But Ossie hadn't really thought it through. If he had he would have known that an equivocal answer to Rolly was as good as a watertight agreement. The following morning Rolly turned up at Ossie's farm even before he had finished the milking. "G'day matey," he said, "I've brought the pig."

Well, Ossie may have been a bit of a battler when it came to running a difficult hillside farm, but battling dangerous inclines, loose rocks and wombat holes was a piece of cake compared with trying to win out over an operator like Rolly Hills. He simply crumbled and sought some kind of refuge in laying down a set of conditions regarding his role as caretaker of the boar. "Okay, Rolly," he said. "I'll look after him for yer ... but only for a few days an' then I want him gone. An' you got to pay me some kind of agistment."

"Good on yer, matey," Rolly said.

He had the back of his trailer down and the pig in Ossie's yard before Ossie had taken his next breath. "He is a pure-bred y'know, Ossie. He come from Pascall's an', as yer know, they breed th' best. Yer can use him on yer sows if yer like."

Ossie was still protesting that the skinny old boar wouldn't be around long enough for that kind of thing even as Rolly was charging off down the lane in a cloud of dust.

As it turned out Ossie was wrong on that point, too. There was ample time for the boar to service all his sows and most of his neighbour's sows twice over if he'd wanted. He didn't see Rolly again for the rest of the winter. Or, to be a little more accurate, those few times he had spotted Rolly in the distance, Rolly had somehow managed to disappear before he could get close enough to hand him the boar's eviction notice.

It wasn't until early in the spring that Rolly showed up in Ossie's farm yard again and Ossie, naturally enough, wasn't all that chuffed to see him. The fact was, in spite of his earlier misgivings about the boar's poor condition and constant cough, it had bloomed on a diet of potatoes and turnips in one of Ossie's sheltered frost-free hill-paddocks. Within a few months it had looked every inch the pedigree boar Rolly had insisted he was. Consequently Ossie had taken the opportunity to run the boar with three of his best sows. The first litter was due any day now and Ossie was waiting expectantly to see what the sow would deliver.

"I'm not sure I want to let him go," he told Rolly. "I mean I've looked after him for yer free for so long now I reckon by rights he's mine."

Rolly bucketed that idea. "Sorry, matey," he said very definitely, "I've already sold him to Denny Bourke up at Hillside. Still, I do appreciate the way he's been looked after. Look, I thought for all yer trouble I'd get yer a nice young sow later. How would that suit?"

It didn't suit Ossie much at all but there seemed very little he could do about it. The boar was, after all, Rolly's. And, as it had turned out, it had been quite useful. But to save some face he resorted to minor threat.

"Okay Rolly," he said. "But you just make sure that sow yer goin' to get me is a good un an' not someone's rubbish, or..."

He didn't quite know 'or what', so he left it there and scowled instead.

Rolly looked hurt at such a suggestion. He clambered back into his old ute and said breezily out the window, "Don' I always look after yer, matey?"

In the face of such a blatant lie Ossie was again stuck for a reply. He took off his hat and scrubbed at his head with his fingers, as if he expected to scratch out a telling retort from his wispy hair and it wasn't until Rolly's dust had cleared at the end of the lane that he thought of it. "No you bloody don't," is what he ought to have said. But by then it was too late so he replaced his battered old hat on his head and settled for a hearty spit instead.

A week later Denny Bourke rang Ossie and asked him about the boar. "They tell me he was your boar an' I'm just checkin'. Rolly suggested he was a pedigree boar in his prime but the way he acts around my sows he gives me the impression he's almost forgot what it's all about. I mean fifty bucks doesn't seem a lot to pay for a pedigree white in his prime."

Ossie recounted as much as he knew about the boar. How he had come by it in the first place and how he had lost it. "I don't know anythin' about him otherwise - except to tell you he ain't no chicken. But in spite of that, Denny, I've got to admit I've got one real nice litter from him already an' two more on the way."

Though his final parting remark was a mite more truculent. "An' I suppose the reason that Rolly can sell him off so cheap is because he boards the bugger out for free."

Denny was a bit placated by Ossie's assurances but nevertheless decided that for the sake of old times he would try and shake Rolly up. Nobody seemed sure who exactly owned the boar and Denny, being a religious man, didn't want to get mixed up in anything that might be a bit shady. Besides, as slow as the boar was, he was pretty sure it had already served his two sows and there didn't seem any good reason to keep it any longer.

That night he rang Rolly and told him he wasn't satisfied with the boar and wanted to talk about getting his money back. To his surprise, Rolly agreed readily. "Sure matey, you've always been a good customer an' I like to keep me customers happy. I'll be around to pick him up as soon as I can. Okay?"

As soon as he could turned out to be three weeks, but as usual Rolly had a good reason for the delay. "Sorry matey," he told Denny Bourke. "I had to help young Tom look after Nola Prate's farm while poor Nola's in hospital havin' her operation."

Denny, for his part, had become a little regretful at his earlier rash decision to have Rolly take the boar back. It had settled in quite nicely and in the warmer weather had even become more sprightly. He suggested to Rolly in all fairness he should keep the pig after all.

Once again, to his surprise, Rolly would have none of it. "No, Denny old matey," he said. "A deal's a deal. I said I'd refund yer money an' I will."

Denny was a bit touched by Rolly's candour. He shook his head. "No, I can't do that, Rolly. I mean, in spite of his initial lack of enthusiasm he's got both my sows in pig an' I feel it's up to me now to sell him off."

Rolly scratched his head and seemed to give Denny's proposal a great deal of consideration before he answered. "Look matey," he said eventually, "I can see yer point, but how about another deal, huh? How about I take the boar off yer hands give yer half yer money back an' in return you can give me a couple of his weaners when they drop? Now I couldn't be fairer than that could I?"

Denny readily agreed to this new arrangement. His two breeding sows rarely had litters under ten piglets. A weaner from each sow would hardly be missed. They shook hands on the deal and Rolly loaded the much travelled boar into his trailer. Four months at Ossie's farm and another few weeks at Denny's place had done the old boy wonders. He really did look in prime condition now. As Rolly drove off he was smiling and waving.

A little too cheery, Denny thought after the dust had settled.

He voiced his suspicions later that evening to his wife. "That rogue Rolly Hills is up to something. I wish I knew what it was."

Which was the same question others were beginning to ask. A few weeks later Denny ran into Colonel Foote at the Post Office. The Colonel pumped him for information about the boar.

"I bought him from Rolly Hills and he told me he was yours, yet now I hear he might have been Ossie Nichols' pig. Someone has to know who he belonged to."

Suspecting some complaint was coming Denny immediately denied any responsibility. "He wasn't my boar," he told the Colonel. "I kind of had him out on licence, if you know what I mean, an' as far as I know it was the same in Ossie's case."

The Colonel looked a little perplexed at that. "So where did Hills get him from? He sold the boar to me. He implied he came from your place and that he was from the Pascall stud. Then later I heard he came from Nichols' place."

Denny shook his head. "I don't know where he came from. I just hope Rolly hasn't pulled another shoofty, that's all. I got two sows in pig to that boar and I'm depending on the fact they're well-bred. I don't want to be feeding mongrel pigs with expensive tucker."

The Colonel allayed his fears. "Oh, he's pedigree alright. A bit old no doubt, but he's Pascall bred, I'll swear. I know them well. I usually get my boars from them but this year I was caught a boar short; so when Hills offered me what I was led to believe was your boar for a hundred dollars, I took him. He'll see the season out and that's all I really wanted."

The two of them eventually parted and went their separate ways still puzzling over the true origin of the old boar and it wasn't until some time later the mystery was solved, but not necessarily aired. It was Pat the barman who got the story out of Rolly one night when Rolly had imbibed a few too many beers. Rolly was shrewd enough, but like most shrewd men he had one weakness - he couldn't help boasting occasionally about his own cleverness.

"They're still yabberin' about that boar, Rolly," Pat said. "The Colonel, Ossie and Denny - it's got 'em obsessed, I reckon."

He leant across the bar and lowered his voice. "C'mon Rolly, you can trust me. You know I can keep a secret. Where did the bugger come from? Yer didn't steal him did yer?"

Rolly laughed. "You know me, matey - I never stole anythin' in me life." He winked broadly. "As a matter of fact he come from the Colonel's in the first place. He reckons he knows a bit about pigs yet he didn't even recognise his own boar."

Pat was puzzled. "How come, Rolly?"

Rolly glanced around quickly to see if anyone was listening and just to be sure he also lowered his voice. "Well, old mate, it's like this - about nine months ago the Colonel rang me an' told me he had this sick boar what I could have for dog meat. He din't want ter chance any general infection, he said. Well, he wasn't that sick - just a bit of a cough an' a loss of condition. I figured a winterin' in a high climate, out of the frost an' fogs an' all, might give him a new spark of life. You know - like them health resorts in Switzerland."

Pat was impressed. He gave a low whistle of admiration. "An' you sold him back to the Colonel for a hundred bucks?"

"Sure I did." Rolly scratched his head thoughtfully. "An' all things considered I reckon it was the best deal I ever made balance-wise. I mean, everybody's happy ain't they. I made a hundred and twenty-five bucks out of an animal I got give to me in the first place. Ossie got three good litters and one of Denny's nice little weaner sows for his trouble, an' young Denny got himself twenty-two of the nicest little pigs you ever saw for a mere twenty-five bucks. An', as fer the Colonel, well I ain't heard any complaints from him either."

Rolly pushed his glass across for a refill and gave Pat another huge wink. "By th' way matey, seein' I also got this real nice little weaner in me shed at home, I suppose you wouldn't by any chance be interested in buyin' a leg of pork in a few weeks time would you?"

"Not in yer bloody life," Pat said as he pushed Rolly's money back across the counter. "Though for a couple of chump chops, matey, you could probably bribe me into keepin' me trap shut."

The Uncertain Burial of Elsa Gernhart

The only property that challenged Ossie Nichols' farm for being the steepest in the district was the Gernhart farm. But whereas Ossie's farm lay on the sunny north-east slopes of the horseshoe range of hills, the Gernhart farm lay on the more shaded southern slopes. Consequently, after heavy rains the steeper roads in the vicinity were often impassable for several days at a time.

Great-grandmother Elsa Gernhart was well aware of this particular problem. Except for a short eight months stint in the city she had always lived in the south hills. She was born not two miles down the road from the Gernhart farm in a pickers' hut during the Depression. Elsa's parents had left the city for the country in search of work. Like the many others wandering around the country in those hard times they hadn't found anything much. In fact the only job Elsa's father could find was some part-time work in an apple orchard. The pay was a mere pittance but the pickers' hut they lived in came free of rent.

With the farmer's consent Elsa's father had fenced off a portion of land and planted a vegetable garden. The produce from the garden, and the rabbits and birds he managed to trap in the nearby blackberry stands, kept them at a kind of subsistence level through the black years of the Depression. Either fortunately or unfortunately, according to one's viewpoint, Elsa turned out to be the only child, a pale-skinned girl whose thinness and lack of colour belied a ropy physical strength and a single-minded determination that, at the tender age of sixteen years, eventually took her off to the city to seek her fortune.

Everyone who knew Elsa thought she was gone for good. It was quite a surprise to everyone in the district when Elsa returned quite unexpectedly a short eight months later. She gave no reason for her early return other than the vague one that living in the city just wasn't worth all the fuss and bother. "A good Christian girl trying to live a quiet and blameless existence in the city was impossible," she said, and left it at that.

Of course, such an answer wasn't really satisfactory to the local gossips who in no time at all had another story to tell. According to them, contrary to Elsa's claim of being a modest Christian girl, she had in fact fallen pregnant the summer before to one of the sons of a valley grazier. One Saturday night instead of dancing like she was supposed to, she was in fact tumbling in the long grass at the back of the dance hall with a rich man's son. According to the gossips, when the worst had become evident, the boy's family had paid for Elsa to go off to the city to have her baby on the quiet and arrange its eventual adoption.

Whether or not the gossips were right in their assumption made no difference to Elsa who never confirmed or denied the rumour. And you could say it didn't make any difference to Henrick when he proposed marriage to Elsa a few months after her return. He was the only son of the Gernharts, who owned one of the most productive dairy farms in the district. That second bit of unexpected news got the gossips going again. It was Henrick this time they had rolling in the grass with Elsa. She's up the duff again. Why else would a strapping young feller like Henrick marry a frail little thing like Elsa who had been starved half of her life?

However, marry they did and, starved or not, Elsa bore five children equally as strapping as their father. A fine crew to run a fine farm. Nevertheless for all that, Elsa Gernhart never lost her reputation for being a little eccentric. You could always expect Elsa to say or do the unexpected. If you asked Elsa Gernhart which she preferred out of lamb or beef she was likely to state her preference for bananas. She was that kind of person. So you could say that nobody was very surprised when they heard that on her eighty-ninth birthday the old lady had decided to go to bed to die. "Eighty-nine's not too bad," she told her relatives and friends, "but ninety's just too damn old. It's time, I reckon, that I joined Henrick."

The Uncertain Burial of Elsa Gernhart

Determined in her cause, she then arranged with Harvey Stone, carpenter and joiner and part-time undertaker, to come to the farm and measure her for her casket. She told him over the phone that she wanted a quick job, too, in case the weather took a turn for the worse. "When I go," she told him, "I want me casket right next to me so's I can be popped straight into it. You'll not find me lyin' around in no shroud waitin' fer the blasted rain to clear."

... she hadn't explained exactly why she needed the extra time away from the worms...

It wasn't really necessary for Harvey to take Elsa Gernhart's measurements; in her old age she was the tiniest of women, slightly less than five feet tall and weighing no more than six and a half stone. Harvey had seen her around the district enough to know she was very definitely an XSSW, so he could have worked from that. But there were other things about the casket that Elsa wanted to discuss, so he arrived as requested and went through the motions of measuring and calculating specific sizes.

Elsa told him she wanted her casket made from her favourite timber, Huon pine. "A Huon pine takes five hundred years to grow to maturity, an' it takes just as long to rot away. It's a matter of time, yer see. A Huon pine casket will keep the worms at bay for as long as I need. The thought of worms crawlin' around in me before then fills me with horror."

Harvey, who had never before made a coffin from Huon pine, thought Elsa's request a little strange because she hadn't explained exactly why she needed the extra time away from the worms. As far as Harvey was concerned, when you were dead you were dead, and the problem of worms was irrelevant. He tried to talk her out of her idea. "Huon pine's hard to get now, Mrs Gernhart, an' hard to work. It's bound to be very expensive."

Elsa told him she didn't give a hang about expense. "I came into this world without anythin' an' that's the way I want to go out of it," she told him. "I'll have that casket if it takes all I got." As proof of her good intent the old lady reached down under her bed and pulled out a large leather-trimmed brocade purse that literally bulged with coins and neat elastic-bound rolls of small denomination bank notes. "It's me pension savin's," she told Harvey. "You build me that casket, Mr Stone, an' you can have every last penny of it. An' when you've built it I want yer to bring it right away into this room so's I'll know it's there ready an' waitin'."

Harvey was used to the final eccentric requests from the older inhabitants of the district so he argued no more and set about his brief energetically. He made a special trip into the city and chose the necessary timber for Elsa's casket. Because there seemed some urgency about the matter, he constructed it within the week and took it up to the Gernhart farm for the old lady's approval.

Propped up in her bed for the occasion, Elsa directed Harvey and his assistant, Percy, to place the casket between two old kitchen chairs under the window. In the light from the window its satin finish glowed with a dull sheen. Harvey walked around the casket looking at it reflectively from different angles. "I only rubbed it with oil, Mrs Gernhart," he said. "I hope that was okay - per'aps it's a bit plain?"

But Elsa would have none of it. She gazed at the casket with a kind of ecstatic admiration and waved his doubts away with one hand as she struggled to reach the bag under her bed with the other. "No no, Mr Stone," she insisted. "You've done very very well. How much do I owe yer?"

Harvey told her the price with some trepidation and Elsa thrust several rolls of notes into his outstretched hand without even taking time to count it.

"Fair go, Mrs Gernhart," Harvey said, "it hasn't got gold fittin's." He counted out his fee and handed her back the change.

Elsa took the bag and dropped it back under her bed without giving it so much as a glance. She was still gazing dreamingly across at her beautiful new-smelling casket as Harvey and Percy quietly left the room.

When her daughter-in-law brought in her tea that evening, Elsa told her of her intention. "I have my casket now," she said in a voice filled with satisfaction and excitement, "so tomorrow I want to say goodbye to everyone." Her daughter-in-law was shocked by the old lady's words and hurried off to tell the rest of the family.

But Elsa had miscalculated. She didn't die. As a matter of fact she lived on for another two and a bit years, though never once in that time did she leave her bed. It was told in the district that her indetermination about dying caused her family some consternation. They dared not leave the old lady for more than a few hours in case she chose that time to go; and yet there was the milking to be done, the crops to be planted, animals to be fed. Elsa was getting to be a bit of a bother.

Towards the end of the second year her son Henry continually complained of his mother's inconsiderateness. "It's jus' too damn disruptin'. I feel obliged to call in every couple of hours no matter what. The farm's beginnin' to suffer. If she don't go soon..." But he didn't dare finish what exactly it was he was threatening to do and none of the others dared to ask.

During her more than two years in bed the members of the family all took their turn keeping the old lady company. Even Ruthie, the youngest member of the family, did her share after school hours. Ruthie was Elsa's great-granddaughter, a serious-minded child who never talked much and was inclined to live in a world of her own making. She didn't really mind looking after her great-gran, whose strange ways captured her imagination. It was just that she hadn't been consulted about it and she let that resentment show with pouted lips and sullen silence.

But as it turned out Ruthie's chore became quite a lucrative one, for in the second week of her stint her great Gran had come to another decision - the old lady had decided her casket was a bit dull after all. She offered Ruthie a handful of money from her bag to mix up a special compound of beeswax, olive oil and essence of lavender. She then directed Ruthie to rub the mixture into the pine casket with a piece of cheesecloth each afternoon. After several weeks of this treatment the coffin looked even more magnificent. Its rich surfaces gleamed gold-brown and butter-smooth, and sometimes, when the light from the window slanted in a particular way, it actually seemed to glow with an almost irresistible, iridescent sheen. Propped up in her bed on the other side of the room, great-grandmother Gernhart took a good deal of pleasure in watching these changes of light and mood. She seemed happier than she had been for many years. The rest of the family thought it ironic - that what had originally been intended as a comfort against the old lady's imminent death was now the very thing that seemed to be keeping her alive.

But Elsa did eventually die, as she had once predicted, during one of the worst summer storms on record. The rain had cascaded down in torrents, onto earth so hot from the previous week's sun that it caused great steamy clouds to constantly swirl through the whole landscape. It was her grandson Billy who found her and remarked, when he ran to get the others, on the eeriness of his discovery. "Damned if the door hadn't blown open ... an' there was fog all through her room. When I found her she was sittin' up in bed, her eyes fixed on that bloody coffin. It's all pretty damn creepy, an' the sooner we get her into it the better as far as I'm concerned," he told them.

The others agreed wholeheartedly. The women of the house prepared Elsa for her final resting place and when she was ready the men popped her into her beloved casket. She fitted in so easily that Billy her grandson was puzzled enough to observe that either Harvey Stone had measured wrong or Gran had shrunk during her two years and a bit in bed. Lying there in the padded powder-blue interior of her beautiful casket she looked no more substantial than an emaciated ventriloquist's doll. Nobody was sorry to see the lid finally closed. All that remained to do now was to arrange for the burial in the town's cemetery. Unfortunately for everyone concerned, that wasn't the end to it, for although the unseasonably heavy rains had stopped, the fogs didn't clear, and in spite of the sticky heat the steep road down to the township remained muddy and impassable for another two days. There was no way the hearse was going to make it up to the farm.

While they waited for the road to dry out the whole family had become increasingly conscious of the once sweet smells of beeswax, pinewood and lavender giving way to the less pleasant smell of Elsa's rapidly disintegrating body. By the morning of the third day since Elsa died it became necessary for those who had to pass Elsa's room to hold a handkerchief soaked in the remainder of Gran's lavender oil over their noses. It was becoming more and more obvious that something had to be done, and it had to be done quickly.

As head of the family it was up to Henry Gernhart to come to some decision. He told the others he was going to ring their neighbour old Willum Haas and ask him to take Gran's coffin out on his cat tractor. "We can arrange for Harvey Stone to bring the hearse an' a hire car to the bottom of the big hill," he told them. "We can follow Willum on foot down that far."

When Willum arrived the men immediately set about loading the coffin on to the back of the tractor, and even though it wasn't an easy task because of its shape, they did finally manage to secure it by sandwiching it between an old door and a mattress. This makeshift structure was then firmly roped to the roll-bar behind Willum's seat. Old Willum removed his hat for the solemn occasion and set the old tractor off down the hill to meet Harvey and his assistant who would be waiting to take Elsa and her coffin straight to the hastily arranged burial ceremony at the cemetery...

When it was told later, nobody seemed to know exactly what went wrong on the way down the hill. Willum didn't, because he was too busy concentrating on not cutting up the road with the heavy tracks of the cat tractor. The Gernharts didn't because they were still preparing to leave the farm house. Only Harvey and his assistant saw it happen but they were too far away to fill in the details. It seems that while Willum was negotiating the second bend Elsa's casket suddenly shot out from between the door and the mattress and careered off down the steepest gully in the district.

"As far as I could see," Harvey said later in Conolly's pub, "it went as quick and slippery as a snake into dry grass down that gully. It even seemed to increase speed as it went, an' no clump of trees could hold it." Harvey also told of the struggle he and Percy had, to climb down into the gully and winkle the casket out of the almost impenetrable scrub and man-ferns. "One side of th' coffin was stove in an' th' top had come off. Poor old Mrs Gernhart had kinda spilled out an' got herself jammed between a couple of rocks."

In a voice bordering on tears he went on to explain how they managed to get the old lady back into the casket and drag it up to the road for some makeshift repairs before the family saw it. "All we had was a few three inch nails an' a blackies' hammer. An', as you might know, Huon pine don't take too kindly to nails. It was a bugger of a job, made worse by the fact Percy here an' me was wet to the skin an' covered in leeches. We had to strip down to our underduds to burn the little buggers off with one of Percy's ciggies. An' jus' to make a bad day go really rotten who should choose that exact time to come slippin' an' slidin' round the corner but the whole of the Gernhart clan. Talk about embarrassin'!"

Nevertheless the funeral took place in the end, even if it was an hour and a half later than scheduled. And the relatives and friends close enough to notice the splits and cracks in the casket didn't bother to complain. All they wanted by that time was for the whole business to be finished with. But unfortunately for the Gernhart family, that coffin caused trouble right to the very end. Even when the last rites had been said and the funeral party was lowering it into the grave, it slipped out of the holding ropes and became jammed sideways between the narrow walls. Henry and Billy had to eventually bash poor Elsa's beautiful Huon pine casket with a crowbar to get it free. Nobody present was sorry to hear the first shovelfuls of earth fall onto the lid.

Harvey Stone swore that if anything like it ever happened again he'd get out of undertaking and go back to making kitchen cabinets. He spent the rest of the night drinking several large beers with whisky chasers and mumbling periodically, in a voice bordering on tears, that it wasn't what old Mrs Gernhart had wanted at all. It was eventually up to Percy, his assistant, to take pity on the rest of the bar and drag his boss off home.

The trauma of the old lady's passing should have been decently forgotten after that terrible day, and it probably would have been, if it hadn't been for young Ruthie who seemed to have picked up many of her great-gran's strange ideas during the period they had spent together. On the way to school one day she suddenly burst into tears when she and her father passed the spot where her great-gran had plummeted into the gully those months before. She was trying to tell her father something but her sobs made it difficult to get the words out. "What's that, Ruthie?" her father asked. "Great-gran's still down there," Ruthie repeated tearfully. "She's still down there jammed in a deep hole between the rocks. The leeches have sucked her dry and now the worms are eating holes in her. Her bones are falling, one by one, deeper an' deeper into the earth. It wasn't her they buried you know ... it was a man-fern."

Billy Gernhart told the story to his wife later that night. "Gawd," he said, "she's a funny imaginative kid. You'd have thought she really believed it."

His wife was nodding in agreement over her knitting when she suddenly stopped and looked up with a very thoughtful expression on her face. "Though come to think of it, Bill," she said with some deliberation, "you did tell us that day that you thought the coffin was very heavy for someone so tiny as your Gran."

Inside a week Harvey Stone was denying the rumour. He insisted that people didn't know what they were talking about. He insisted that Huon pine weighted heavy and that's all there was to it. But it also must be told that after Elsa Gernhart's unlikely burial Harvey Stone was never quite the same again. I suppose you could say he began to fear death.

He became glum and morose every time he heard someone was on their death bed. It wasn't the right attitude at all for someone running an undertaking business. Nobody in the town was too surprised when a few months after Elsa Gernhart's burial he finally sold out his undertaking business and went back to making cupboards and cabinets as he had threatened to do.

"I'll make anythin' yer want me to make," he told prospective customers glumly, "as long as yer don't want it made outa Huon bloody pine!"

Whisky Wedding

When Kev Parker returned to the Montvale district some twelve years after he'd left it with his small inheritance, he returned a relatively wealthy man. This turnabout was somewhat of a shock to the many in the past who had proclaimed that Kev would one day finish up on a city park bench, homeless and broke. Kev was by far the district's worst boozer and there was no reason for them to think Kev's move to the city would do anything to break the habit of a lifetime. The opposite really, most proclaimed; there were many pubs in the city and many publicans who would be only too willing to encourage a no-hoper like Kev to drink his money away in their pub. Give him a bar corner with a racing form guide for company, they said, and he'd drink as much in an afternoon's racing time as the average man would drink in a week.

Some had even gone to the trouble to work out in time/drinking-cost terms how it would only be four to five years before Kev hit the poverty wall, a reasonable prediction one would have thought in the circumstances; and yet, much to the suppressed chagrin of those who had predicted his early downfall, here he was again, in his home pub, brighter and more cheerful than ever, not in the least looking like park-bench material and willing to tell without restriction to all those who would listen, how his good fortune had come about.

"It doesn't take a lot of brains getting rich," he told them. "All you gotta do is sit in the right places an' keep y'ears open. The right place for me was the back bars of those city pubs where the horse racing fraternity congregated. I drank and I listened. I listened in to jockeys discussin' jockeys, horse owners discussin' horses and bookies discussin' the odds. I soon found out who and what was trying for which race and who was looking for a better handicap for the Big One."

According to Kev, the combination of this valuable information judiciously used in the betting shops and the phenomenal luck he'd had since childhood eventually won him enough money to buy a half share in a thoroughbred trotter which, in another streak of good fortune, turned out to be something of a champion. From that time on Kev went from success to success, until he owned an equal share in one of the best little stables of trotters in the state.

So why had Kev quit? He told the bar in Conolly's pub that his business just got too big to handle. "Too much sweat and worry. Too much to think about. Too many people to watch," he told them. "It was all beginning to interfere with me drinking time so I decided to chuck it all in and retire to the life of a jolly squatter."

A few weeks after his return Kev Parker bought a small parcel of very desirable land with an unsurpassed view of the valley where he was born and set about organising the building of his new house. Pretentious rather than comely, it was the kind of house which screamed material success. And just to rub a little more salt into the wounds of all those who predicted his downfall he added his own personal touch by directing the builder to incorporate a feature archway between the dining room and the living room made from two and a half thousand empty beer bottles. As much a salute to his wayward and profitable past as it was a celebration of his future intention.

But unbeknown to Kev there was also some danger in making such a big splash. Not only had the completion of his house designated him a truly successful man, it had also, in one fell swoop - and not withstanding his propensity to put away prodigious amounts of grog - also designated him the district's most desirable bachelor. He had built the nest and it soon became evident to himself as well as everyone else that there were many potential mates, not only willing, but anxious, to share it with him.

In spite of the dire warnings from all those who could remember Kev's wanton past, there was an immediate and pronounced shuffling to the fore from the eligible single women in the district who saw Kev as a possible saviour, someone who could take them away from the drudgery of being a shop assistant or domestic help for the rest of their lives, someone who might be able to alleviate not only their financial stress but to some degree their loneliness as well.

To those who aspired to become his mate, Kev Parker was still a boozer of course, but deep in their collective bosoms there was the undying optimism that, having once set themselves up in Kev's brick and tile mansion, they could reform this one undesirable aspect of a man who was, by all reports, timid and self-effacing. It wouldn't be too hard, they thought, to change his unrestrained boozing into a more acceptable restrained social drinking. It was only a matter of the right nurturing.

Consequently when Kev advertised in the local paper for a live-in cook/housekeeper he was a bit appalled by the number of applicants of various ages who fronted up for the position, and the manner in which they presented themselves. Most of the fourteen applicants were dressed to the nines. They reeked of cheap perfumes which, in spite of their primary intention, smelt more like a barber's shop than a boudoir. Many of them could have been potential candidates for Show Girl of the Year rather than applicants for a job as cook/housekeeper.

Hair piled on top of their heads, or teased and curled into intricate styles, they pranced excitedly from room to room, sighing heavily and ecstatically each time they came across yet another marvel of modern design. High heels digging holes in the shag pile carpet, eyes flashing here and there, they searched out first the bathrooms and then the bedrooms. Some of them even went as far as laying hands tentatively on beds and exclaiming in hushed excited tones of their comfort and springiness. Their overtly friendly banter, their constant eye-fluttering and head-tossing as they parried Kev's half-hearted questions with high tinkling laughter, reminded him rather disconcertingly of some of the mares and fillies he'd once owned when they began anticipating the mating season.

"None of that lot even got as far as the kitchen," Kev later remarked ruefully to Pat the barman in Conolly's hotel. "They seemed more intent on sussin' out the good life than discussin' the fundamentals of cookin' and cleanin'."

Others again, of the more cerebral variety, had apparently come with words of encouragement and wisdom that would have done credit to experienced social workers. That group talked about like interests and compatibility, healthy diets and the relative merits of positive thinking. Rather than a close examination of the house they seemed more interested in wandering through the newly landscaped garden. Their conversation was restricted to the concepts of harmony and inspiration rather than the more mundane things Kev was offering, like better than average wages and lighter than average duties. It was all very disturbing to someone like Kev who had, in his entire forty-four years of life, only ever had one dalliance with the opposite sex and then more by accident than design.

He eventually got around to interviewing Sara Maney, the buxom and not so young widow of a tree-feller who had sadly miscalculated the wind direction two years before. Sara was the only one of the fourteen applicants dressed as if she meant business. She also, either by accident or good sense, arrived with her two well-scrubbed and well-behaved children. Sara settled them down with their books on Kev's balcony, and inside Kev's well-appointed kitchen she talked of nothing else but the relative merits of wall ovens, vacuum cleaners, roast dinners and apple pies.

Kev took as much note of the two children still quietly reading on the balcony as he did of Sara's strong and capable hands as she turned switches on and off, exclaiming all the while of her unrestrained admiration for the entire house and its effects. He was grateful that she, at least, seemed to understand what it was he really wanted.

Much to the vexation of the remainder of the unattached females in the district, who seemed to consider that because Sara had already had a go at living with a man it was now someone else's turn, Kev hired Sara on the spot. They made arrangements that she would begin her housekeeping duties the following week. As a gesture of goodwill Kev rang for a taxi from the town to take her and her children home. He then gratefully retired to his study (which was in fact his own private barroom) and opened up his wall cocktail cabinet to celebrate his continuing good fortune with a bottle of his favourite Scotch whisky.

Within a very short time of her taking up the job, Sara Maney had Kev's new house running like clock-work. Meals were always on time. The house (except for Kev's study which only he was allowed into) was kept spotless, as were her two children who, at the ages of eight and nine, should have been loud and raucous but weren't. They were always on their best behaviour. Kev couldn't have been more satisfied with his good sense (or was it more of his good luck) in choosing Sara. He settled himself down to a quiet and peaceful early retirement.

As it turned out Sara Maney had much the same designs on Kev as the other hopefuls who had turned up that day but Sara, being a woman of greater experience when it came to men, was a mite more subtle, certainly more patient in her approach. She made her move three months later.

By that time the routine of the house was well and truly fixed. Each day Kev would get up after the children had gone to school, have his shower, dress and stroll down to the kitchen where Sara would cook his favourite breakfast of bacon and eggs, devilled kidneys or savoury mince on toast. After he had eaten his breakfast it was his habit to sit out on the terrace under the sun umbrella for most of the morning, reading up on his latest horseracing guides.

At midday Sara would bring him a light lunch; sometimes a Danish open sandwich, sometimes a slice of quiche with vegetables, sometimes something else; but whatever it was, it was always on time and it was always tasty. Mostly he and Sara ate their lunch together on the terrace and she would question him about his childhood, or his life on the racing circuit. After lunch was finished Kev would ring for the taxi and go to the pub where he would spend a convivial afternoon and evening in a state of constant intoxication as he indulged in his second favourite pastime of betting on the gee-gees, though never more than a few dollars at a time, because he had no intention of losing any of his "lucky" money. If he won (which he often did) he was happy, and if he lost he couldn't have cared less. At closing time, when he was boozed to the eyeballs, his taxi would be waiting to take him home. If he had won that day his practice was to shout the bar and give the barman and cab driver a generous tip because he wanted others to share in his good fortune. All around, Kev found that his popularity, in spite of the fact he was still putting away more grog in the day than the average wharfie could in a week, was on the rise. Life was truly sweet and just the way he had always dreamed it could be.

Until, that was, Sara put in her notice. She told him she wasn't quitting the job because she was dissatisfied, she said it was for the sake of her and her children's respectability. "You wouldn't know it," she told him, "because you don't hear the gossip like I do. Half the female population in the district are talking about us. I've tried to ignore it myself but for the sake of the children I'm afraid I can't any longer. At school the other kids are forever callin' the poor little things names."

Kev was shocked. He knew there were many who continued to disapprove of his lifestyle and weren't loath to chatter about it behind his back, but to bring such a kind and respectable person like Sara Maney and her well-behaved children into it was too much.

"Don't you worry Sara," he told her, "I'll have it out with them. If I hear anybody talkin' about either of us I'll sue 'em as quick as yer can spit."

Sara shook her head sadly. "It won't do any good, Mr Parker. You know what it's like, there's never anything said out in the open."

When Kev thought how his near perfect life was in danger of collapsing round his ears he began to panic. There was no way he was going to get another gem of a housekeeper like Sara.

"Look," he said recklessly, "I'll double yer money. I can afford it."

Sara smiled gratefully. "It's nice of you to offer, Mr Parker, but I'm afraid that won't stop them suggesting that the two of us are living in sin. And us being Catholics and all - I'm sorry, I really am."

Kev was at a loss to understand it all. In all his life he'd never said anything nasty about anyone else and couldn't understand how others could do it. "But it's not true," he protested. "How could anyone say it is?"

"People don't always do what's right," she said, "they do what's proper. And proper in Montvale is not to live in the same house as an unmarried man."

"Gawd," Kev said dismally. "There must be somethin' we can do to shut 'em up." He even suggested he could buy her a little house nearby so she could come in each day.

Sara raised her eyebrows at that suggestion. "They'd only say I was a kept woman then, Mr Parker. No, I'm sorry, there's no alternative, me and the kids will have to go." She leaned forward and gave him a quick affectionate pat of consolation on his arm. "But don't you worry, Mr Parker, a nice man like you will have no trouble in getting someone else to look after your lovely house."

Poor Kev. He didn't want someone else. He wanted things to stay just as they were and that wasn't going to happen. It seemed like his luck had finally gone bad. All that day he wandered around in the semi-dazed state of a man in mourning. He even broke with his habit of going to the pub and instead stayed in his study consuming vast amounts of whisky and beer. But it didn't help at all. He just became more and more miserable. By the time he staggered off to bed that night he had made up his mind what to do. He stopped outside Sara's bedroom door and gave it a tentative knock. Sara opened her door. She was dressed only in her nightie. The light by her bed was on and Kev was a little appalled to realise he could see right through the flimsy material. She could have been standing there stark naked.

In his confusion he blurted out his proposition. "I could marry you," he told a surprised Sara. "We could get married an' carry on just as before. Instead of payin' you a wage I'll arrange for an allowance for you and the kids ... I'll leave everythin' to you in my will ... I won't ask you for anythin' ... I mean, we'll still keep our own bedrooms an' all. It'll be just like it is now. What d'you reckon?"

Was there a slight change in Sara's expression? Did a tiny light flicker in her eyes? It was hard to say. She stood there for a second or two leaning almost casually against the doorstop and Kev suddenly thought he might have gone too far. A respectable woman like Sara marrying the district's worst boozer. It suddenly seemed to him his proposition was incredibly out of order.

"I'm s..sorry," he said hastily. "I thought it might work ... you know." He gave her a slightly apologetic smile and steadied himself in readiness to stagger off towards his own bedroom.

"It's very nice of you Mr Parker," she said eventually, "but I don't want charity, you know."

Poor Kev was even more embarrassed. How could he have been so stupid?

"No, I didn't mean that ... I meant ... I thought it might suit everyone. Quieten the gossips ... you know."

Sara looked thoughtful for a moment. "I suppose it would solve a lot of things ... I mean the kids and all - not having a father."

To Kev's relief she smiled suddenly. "Okay Kevin," she said suddenly. "You're on. We'll talk about it in the morning."

She gave him a quick nod and closed the door abruptly in his face, leaving him swaying irresolutely in the hallway. He hadn't really expected such a definite response. As he staggered off to his own bedroom that night he felt a rising sense of panic again. Had he been unduly reckless? Had he put all his day's winnings on a rank outsider without knowing the filly's real form? His dreams that night were chock-a-block full of flying hooves bearing down on him, turf flying into his face, sticking mud and greasy grass. There was nowhere to escape but into further confusion...

By the late afternoon of the following day the word had got around the district. Kev didn't know how it had happened but Sara certainly did. She had told Phylis Barnes the baker's wife when she had bought the bread that morning - and that was enough.

"He's goin' to make an honest woman of me," she had whispered confidingly. "We thought it best in the circumstances ... you know, what with the gossip an' all."

In fact Phylis Barnes hadn't been aware of any gossip, which was very unusual seeing she was the source of most of it. Her very next customer was Dulcie Hills who carried the news to Spratt's bootery and from that time on the news spread like wildfire.

"Someone's gone crazy," Mrs Spratt said to the postmaster, "but I'm not sure who."

During the period between his proposal and the wedding Kev lived in a kind of alcoholic daze. His demeanour fluctuated between hope and despair. The eventual outcome of his mixed feelings was that, while Sara prepared herself for the wedding by ordering from the shops all those things she considered necessary for a pleasant nuptial life, Kev's preparations took on the aspirations of one of history's greatest binges.

"I don't mind anythin' when I'm drunk," he told Pat the barman one afternoon. "It's only when I'm sober that I ask myself the questions."

Not surprisingly, Kev's extra heavy drinking could have caused Sara much vexation, but it didn't. Smart woman that she was, she had predicted it was quite on the cards that Kev might well make a fool of them

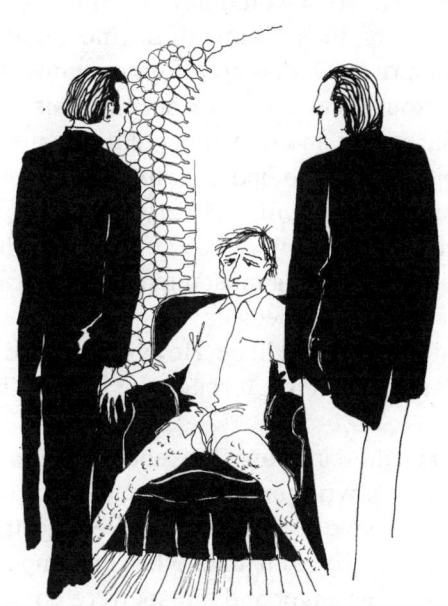

"No bugger's gonna welsh out on our sister's weddin', Kev."

both on their wedding day, so she took out insurance on that possibility by raiding Kev's cocktail cabinet the day before the wedding was due to take place. She swept up the entire contents and hid them while Kev was down at the pub.

And later that night when he was snoring off the consequences of another heavy day's drinking she pulled the plugs on the two phones and raided his closet too. The two phones, his suits, his shirts, his ties, his socks, all followed the way of the whisky, the rum, the liqueurs, the gins and the wines.

But, as it turned out, her plan to make sure Kev couldn't get at any grog until the wedding was over wasn't all that effective. Pulling such a rotten trick on anyone would have been fraught with difficulty, but pulling it on Kev, on the morning of the most traumatic day of his life, was bound to turn out a disaster of momentous proportions. Kev did not have the resources to cope with such a crisis.

The moment he awoke and remembered it was his wedding day he headed for his grog store only to find it as empty as old Mother Hubbard's cupboard. No phone to ring home delivery. No clothes to tramp down the road in. To put it mildly, Kev well and truly flipped his lid. He ranted and raved around the house in a most uncharacteristic manner, turning out cupboards, looking under beds, in the washing machine, anywhere he thought his lost property might be. He even checked out the goldfish pond in the garden and searched through the garden sheds looking for his grog.

In his pyjamas and dressing gown he wandered like a lost soul through the rooms of his house, wringing his hands and swearing in a terrible manner. He seemed to have no interest whatever in getting ready for the wedding, let alone getting there on time. When his temper receded enough for him to realise that his anger and threats were not going to have the desired effect of having Sara reveal where she had hidden the grog, he finally resorted to pleading and tears, and eventually, to non-cooperation. He slumped deep in his chair and refused to budge. "Okay," he said. "No grog, no weddin'."

Sara countered. "No weddin', no grog."

It was stalemate.

Even when Sara's two brothers arrived with the hire cars to pick them up, Kev was still sitting there, white, trembling, but adamant. He pointed a shaking finger at Sara. "You can take her to the church," he told them. "But I'm not goin'. I've changed me mind."

Michael, the eldest of the two brothers glared down at him threateningly, fists clenching and unclenching. "No bugger's gonna welsh out on our sister's weddin', Kev."

In spite of the implied threat Kev still stuck to his guns. Such was the agony of his sobriety a broken nose would have been easier to bear. "I'm not goin' an' that's all there is to it. I don't care if you beat the shit out of me. I not goin' anywhere without a drink."

But Kev was wrong. Born of elderly parents he was a bit of a runt and in spite of his furious struggles Sara's two hefty brothers managed to manhandle him into his wedding clothes which had appeared almost miraculously from out of nowhere. They carried him to one of the cars and dumped him in. As they charged off down the road, Michael told Kev of their plan with the firm-jawed assurance of a man strictly in charge.

"Right Kev, we get dropped off at the church while our brother Seamus here goes back for Sara and the littlies. But don't you worry about anything at the church, ay? I'll be right alongside you all the way."

The Maney clan thought they had the situation under control but they were wrong. Kev might not have been too strong physically but his years of punting with race-course touts, pub bookies, and temperamental horses had taught him the value of not being seen as a sucker. Stubborn's one thing, determination's another. So, as they say, you can lead a man to the altar but you can't make him say "I do". Not, that is, if he's determined not to.

The result was, that when it came time for Kev to answer in the affirmative he refused to say it. He just stood there in front of the gathered well-wishers staring belligerently at the priest. The situation was even more embarrassing for Sara than it would have been if he'd been rolling drunk and incoherent.

She could hear the beginnings of wonder and impatience, and possibly mirth, in the shuffling and whisperings of her relatives and friends behind her back. It was time for compromise. She asked the priest's indulgence for a moment and drew Kev aside. "Okay Kevin," she hissed, "let's make a bargain. You go through with the ceremony and I'll promise to get you a drink as soon as we get in the car."

Kev thought about it for a bit. He knew that at the moment he had the upper hand but he also knew that the consequence of not going through the wedding at all was, to say the least, alarming. "You swear you'll do that?"

"I swear it," Sara answered.

Kev sighed. He could already feel the smooth touch of liquor sliding down his throat. "Okay," he said in a very dry whisper. "It's a deal. Lead me to the altar an' let's make it as quick as possible."

So, much to everyone's relief, the ceremony was completed, the rice and confetti thrown, the pictures taken, the kissing and hand-shaking concluded. Once back in the car, true to her word, Sara produced a flask of whisky from her purse and handed it across to him. She gave her new husband just the hint of a smile as she watched him lift the flask to his lips and practically drain its contents in one swallow. "I thought it might come to this," she said.

By the time they got to the R.S.L. hall for the reception Kev had almost recovered his usual good spirits. And even though at times he gave the impression of being as thirsty as a two-headed tin dog in a desert, and consequently was inclined to slur his words and fall about a bit, his behaviour was otherwise exemplary.

He was constantly on the move, passing out plates of food and filling half empty glasses; and then later, when it came time for his speech, he delighted all those present with a series of hilarious (and mostly made-up) experiences in the racing game that had many of those present rolling in the aisles. Even the taciturn Herbie Miles was eventually inspired enough to raise his glass and propose a toast to Kev as the most popular bridegroom of the year. Not one of those present failed to raise their glass in ready response.

Later in the evening, and in somewhat different circumstances than earlier, Sara's two brothers picked him up and carried him to one of the cars. They drove him home and helped Sara put him to bed. After her brothers had gone Sara collected up Kev's belongings, which she'd hidden amongst her underwear in the bottom of her very generous glory box, and replaced them in their rightful places; the clothing to Kev's wardrobe, the phones plugged back in their sockets and the bottles of grog into Kev's walnut-veneer cocktail cabinet. And tomorrow, she thought, I cook him his favourite breakfast just like before.

And just to show she was as sensible as she was kind-hearted, she made a vow that night about Kev's impossible drinking habit. Wise woman that she was, she vowed that she would let Kev go his own way in the future; and that one of her most important wifely duties would be to make sure that Kev's cabinet was always well stocked.

Until, that was, cirrhosis of the liver did them part!

Nothing But the Best

When his much loved dog Flash died, Harold Bushell decided to invest in a really good sheep dog to replace him. He didn't have the time or the patience to train a pup himself so he reckoned he'd buy an already trained dog from a professional dog-trainer. "It'll cost me an arm and a leg but another well-trained dog like Flash'll make my life a lot easier," Harold told his wife and son at breakfast one morning.

They both readily agreed. Having in the past suffered from Harold's many tantrums with half-trained dogs, they were only too willing to encourage this unlikely splurge of Harold's in any way they could. As far as Harold's family was concerned, the two years he'd had his beloved Flash by his side was the only time they could remember there being any kind of truce between Harold and the farm animals. Many times Mrs Bushell was heard to express her view that her Harold was not "temper'mentally" suited to farming. "Machinery's more in Harold's line - somethin' without legs that doesn't grunt, moo, or bleat," she said.

It was also a fact that Harold had been warned by the local doctor that he wasn't to over-excite himself because his blood pressure was higher than it should have been. Less worry and less work, was the quack's advice, so his buying a well-trained dog to replace poor old Flash seemed the best way of achieving both of those directives.

It was Harold's wife who first saw the advertisement in the daily paper. She pointed it out to her husband when he came back from his contract fencing job that evening. Harold pored over the ad for a few minutes, mumbling the words and phrases like he might have been addressing a prayer to the almighty. "Young ... expertly trained ... boundless energy ... friendly."

"He sounds like a real little beauty," he said finally. "I think I might go an' look him over t'morrow. I can finish Nola's fence next week. I'm not goin' to buy an expensive dog without a real good trial."

"If they can't muster a chicken into a tin bucket before they're a year old, they're out..."

It was easy to see by Harold's uncharacteristic enthusiasm that he was already stuck on the idea, and the upshot was he rang the phone number the ad gave and arranged to see the dog in action the following day. But, in spite of his enthusiasm about buying a trained sheep dog,

Harold was also a cautious man, especially when it came to parting with hard-earned money.

"I'll leave at first light tomorra," he told his wife. "It'll give me plenty of time then to check around the town where this feller lives to see what I can find out about him an' his dog before I commit meself."

Harold arrived the next morning just as the pub opened, and over a quiet beer in the public bar he set about making a few discreet enquiries about the advertised dog's owner.

"Sure," one of the locals told him, "Bart Thomas is the best man with dogs around these parts, there's no question about that."

Other townspeople he quizzed readily agreed with this statement. It seemed that Bart Thomas was a dog-trainer of the highest repute. That was good enough for Harold. He finished his beer and set out to have a closer look at the dog itself.

Bart Thomas' house sat back from the road on the outskirts of the town. Even as Harold drove his ute into Bart's yard he was verifying in his mind all the good things he had been told in the local pub about the man. Harold had never seen such a well organised set-up. He counted at least seven dogs in the yard and each one had its own special shed and concrete enclosure, and every one was spotlessly clean. Neither did the dogs set up an unholy row as Harold drove into the yard. There was a kind of muted greeting from the dogs but nothing more spectacular than that.

It seemed, Harold thought, almost as though the dogs had been told there was a potential buyer coming and that they had to be on their best behaviour. Harold was greatly impressed, and when Bart came to greet him he told him so.

Bart Thomas nodded, taking the compliment in his stride, as he began immediately to explain why his dogs were the best. "It's not only a matter of trainin' yer know - they've got to be the right strain. My dogs go back eight generations an' I've only ever kept th' best to breed from. Courage, loyalty, strength, obedience an' persistence is second nature to 'em. An' when it comes to workin', my dogs are machines."

Considering all he'd seen and heard, Harold couldn't wait to see one of these super-dogs in action but he didn't want to appear too anxious just in case Bart took advantage and upped the ante. "Which one's fer sale then?" he asked Bart as off-handedly as he could. But he couldn't, in the end, keep his voice from cracking slightly with the effort. He resorted to a quick cough into his hand with the hope Bart would interpret it as an indication he wanted to get on with the business rather than as a sign of the excitement he truly felt.

Bart led him across the yard to one of the cages and opened the gate. A fine-looking black and white border collie bounded out and sat looking up at the man expectantly, his whole body quivering with anticipation. Harold wasn't quite sure whether the dog was waiting for a pat or an order. The dog got neither. Not as such, anyway. The flick of Bart's two fingers was hardly discernible. It was as if the dog sensed rather than saw what was required of him. From a sitting position the dog suddenly leaped fully four feet in the air and landed as neat as you like in the centre of Harold's ute.

"Righty-o, now I'll show you what he can do," Bart said with the same casualness Harold had intended for himself earlier. Only Harold had to admit in Bart's case there was no hint of anything other than complete unbridled confidence.

The dog's owner pointed back down the road. "I've got three or four sheep in the killin' paddock down by the river. Take us down there an' I'll put him to work."

"He's certainly fit," Harold said for want of something better to say as they drove off down the road. He was already infatuated by the whole proceedings and was calculating in his mind the highest price he could go to.

"Nifty as a mallee bull," his companion agreed, "an' quicker than a hawk as well."

He got Harold to stop by a long thin paddock that curved across the top of a small hill. In the distance Harold could see the sweep of willow tops and the glint of a river. There wasn't a sign of any sheep.

Bart climbed out of the ute, took his hat off, looked at the sky for a moment then whacked his hat across his knee. Perhaps that was the signal to the dog, perhaps not, Harold wasn't at all sure. What was certain was the speed at which the dog shot from the back of the ute and disappeared over the brow of the hill. A trained greyhound couldn't have moved any quicker, and then before Harold even had time to hide his further admiration behind his handkerchief, the dog was back, driving the small mob of sheep before him at a relentless speed.

Bart whistled suddenly and the dog dropped so flat it almost disappeared from sight in the dry grass. Then, with a series of whistles and hand movements, Bart had the dog moving first left, then right, forwards and backwards, circling and flattening again with such ease and precision it seemed to Harold as though Bart was the ballet master and the dog and the sheep the chorus dancing to his instructions.

Eventually there was nowhere for the sheep to go but into a tight circle at the top corner of the paddock where the ute was parked. Such was his concentration during the demonstration that Harold forgot all about the need to retain his cool aloofness. He was transfixed, standing half in and half out of the ute door; and to make matters worse his jaw dropped open and his eyes had a kind of fixed intensity that could have been construed as the look of a stunned mullet.

Bart had remarked earlier that when it came to work his dogs were machines, but this demonstration seemed to deny anything so ordinary as mechanics. The way man and dog had worked to such perfection with the absolute minimum of effort seemed to Harold to be more in the line of mental telepathy. The dog had often responded so quickly there hadn't been time for any order to be fully given. To say the very least, Harold was enthralled. He heard Bart's voice intruding into his thoughts, it seemed to be coming from a great distance.

"Well? How about that, ay?"

Harold could only nod his head vigorously in mute appreciation. There seemed little he could say that would have added anything worthwhile. As good as old Flash had been, he was still an amateur compared with this amazing dog.

"I start trainin' 'em when they're no more than eight weeks old," Bart told him. "If they can't muster a chicken into a tin bucket before they're a year old, they're out. I only keep the very best."

By this time Harold was certain he wanted that dog no matter what the price. He envisaged a much easier life in the future. No more screaming at half-trained dogs. No more high blood pressure. He'd be the envy of every farmer in the Montvale district.

But Bart wasn't finished yet. "He can also work as wide as yer like," he said. He clicked his fingers and the dog bounded towards Bart's feet, where it sat quivering, head raised expectantly. The sheep, suddenly finding themselves free to wander again, began moving off up the slope of the paddock.

Bart kept Harold talking until the sheep had disappeared over the brow of the hill and then he took his hat off and gave it a quick twirl behind his back. The dog jumped to his feet and charged off through the fence behind them and dived into a thick clump of ferns. A few seconds later Harold saw it flash across a hill a paddock away heading in the general direction the sheep had taken earlier. He watched, fascinated, as the dog passed through the middle of a large mob of cattle with such speed they hardly had time to look up in fright.

"Nothin' distracts him," Bart said airily, "not even a bitch on heat."

Not more than a minute later the sheep reappeared over the hill with the dog following at a discreet distance. As the sheep moved closer to the two men, the dog narrowed the gap between itself and the sheep until it was only a pace or two away from the sheep's rumps.

"Now watch this," Bart said as he raised his hat and with arm outstretched he wriggled it about like an cricket umpire signalling a no-ball. The dog leapt right over the top of the sheep and stopped them dead in their tracks. He stood there motionless for a while, staring into their faces, then slowly he began to circle until the sheep were in a tight little pack a short distance from the fence.

"Go and get one of 'em," Bart said. "He'll hold 'em there until they all bloody starve to death if yer want."

Harold was not only sold, he was ecstatic with the prospect of owning such a dog. He nodded his head. He had seen enough. "I'll take him," he said.

"You realise he don't come cheap," Bart said.

Harold's mind was made up. "I'll take him," he repeated. He very nearly said at any price but checked himself with an effort. Bart seemed the sort of bloke who might take advantage of a besotted purchaser...

Harold didn't get back to his farm until quite late. His wife and son had finished the milking and it was coming on to dark. Such was his suppressed excitement he hardly ate his hot dinner, and later when he finally went to bed, his sleep was full of snorts, grunts and chuckles.

At first light he insisted they all go down to the sheep paddock to try the dog out. All the way down the lane Harold preached the dog's ability. "I've never seen a dog like him around here. Or for that matter anywhere. I've decided to call him Lightnin'. Here, watch..."

Harold removed the lead from the dog's collar, raised his arm in the general direction of the ewes and snapped his fingers. The dog disappeared into the ferns as quick as the flick of a fly's wing. They had a brief glimpse of him on the outskirts of the mob and in less time than it takes to spit he was back - driving three ewes relentlessly before him.

Harold couldn't believe his eyes. "Go back you bastard an' get th' rest," he shouted hoarsely. In no time at all the dog was back with another three ewes.

At this point Harold seemed in danger of having a heart attack right then and there in the middle of the paddock. His usual ruddy complexion had deepened several shades to the colour of bottled red beet.

As his son commented later, "I thought the old boy was gunner burst inter flames." He and his mother had left Harold eventually. They couldn't stand to witness such agony any longer. They decided it was best not to try to reason with him, but just to leave him there to work it out of his system and hope he did so before his heart exploded.

Come dark that night, Harold was still down in the ewe paddock trying to break the dog's jaundiced view of how many ewes it took to make up the ideal sized mob. When he did finally return to the farmhouse he didn't want to talk about it - other, that was, than to state with some triumph that at least twice he had managed to get the dog to bring up five sheep at one time.

"An' by gawd," he said, "he'll do better than that if it takes me the rest of me life."

The problem was, of course, that Harold had bought himself a trial dog and in trials a dog usually only has to work three sheep. There was no doubt the dog was good but he wasn't quite the champion Harold had thought. A point, incidentally, that was revealed later when one of the stock agents recognised the dog as a Thomas dog.

"He just missed out on winning the state championships twice in a row," the agent told Harold.

"Yeah," Harold said dismally. "An' that bugger Bart Thomas only keeps the best, I know."

Nevertheless Harold, being the stubborn type, was determined to make the best of it, and six months later he had managed to get the black and white dog to work nine sheep. The problem was, it took a long time for Harold to muster his sheep and rather than him finding life easier with a well-trained dog, he found it considerably more difficult. Everyone reckoned it wasn't doing his blood pressure much good either.

Scorpio Rising

Sergeant Tom Plaister had been in the district several years. At the age of fifty-two he no longer had any ambition to get promoted. He felt that if he kept his head down and did a reasonable job his bosses would leave him alone until his retirement. Unfortunately that wasn't the way it happened in the end and he only had himself and another man's obsession to blame.

Tom Plaister had joined the police force at the age of nineteen, looking, he said, for adventure. But after several years of patrolling freeways, arresting drunken drivers and becoming embroiled in the domestic arguments of suburbia, all he wanted was a change; so, when the chance for a promotion and transfer to a country station came his way, he took it. He considered that a year or two in the country would do no harm before he made his next bid to climb up the promotional ladder.

Much to his surprise, he liked the quiet country life. He found it much more to his taste than the city. Not that there wasn't your average share of lawbreakers in the country, it was just that the crimes there were more benign. A quiet warning in private was usually enough to put the frighteners onto those he suspected of indulging in a bit of sheep duffing or spud bandicooting. Or in the case of the younger fry, an unexpected patrol around the town was usually threat enough to send all but the most recalcitrant scuttling off home.

The sergeant even surprised himself further by becoming a keen gardener, an avid fly fishermen, a rider of horses and an occasional shooter of rabbits and wild ducks. All of which, one way or another, became acceptable substitutes for his original desire for adventure.

Thus, after a time, his machinations on the promotional ladder became somewhat erratic. Rather than seeking out a post that might further his professional ambitions, he was more inclined to keep his eye open for the country station that best suited his off-duty interests.

His last transfer was to the Montvale district where a modern police station with flat attached had just been built. There was enough ground out the back for a generous garden, rivers and lakes aplenty where he could indulge in his two favourite sports and plenty of horses for hire when he wanted one. He made up his mind. It suited him fine. He'd be there until his retirement.

It also should be said he was a reasonably happily married man. He had married quite young, to a civilian clerk who worked at the city station he had been attached to. They had two grown-up children and three lovely little grandchildren. All in all the local sergeant was pleased with his life.

It wasn't until his wife went on a trip to New Zealand to visit her sick sister that his troubles began. Tom Plaister was suddenly a bachelor, a state he had barely experienced before, seeing he had got married only eighteen months out of police training school. As a cook he was abysmal. He could, as they say, char a slice of toast, boil an egg and make a pot of tea but that was about it.

Mrs Plaister, knowing her husband's culinary shortcomings, suggested she try to arrange for a part-time housekeeper to look after him in the time she'd be away. The sergeant would have none of that. Too costly by half, he told her. He assured her he would be okay on his own - a foolish assurance he came to regret the very day he ran out of the prepared meals his wife had solicitously packed into the freezer.

Consequently, he had to start looking a little further afield for his food, and the best source of the already cooked variety was the local bakery where he bought his bread, cakes and pies for his evening meals from the amiable and loquacious Phylis Barnes, the baker's wife. Sympathetic to his plight, Phylis suggested if he could manage to get his own breakfast, she would prepare him a packet of sandwiches or muffins for his lunch each day, and he could have his evening meals at the pub.

Eventually, this innocent arrangement with Phylis Barnes took on a somewhat greater complexity when, in gratitude to her kind consideration for keeping his pies nicely hot and filling his sandwiches and muffins more lavishly than ordinary commerce demanded, he began to bring her a freshly caught fish, or a fat bunny for her table. And, as one thing led to another, it wasn't very long before he was being invited home by Phylis (once her husband had gone off for the night's baking, that was) to see just how nice a fresh, brown trout, pan fried in garlic butter, or a baked rabbit stuffed with olives could be.

Everybody in the township seemed to know and accept Phylis' on-off affairs. It was almost like she was a single woman anyway, given that she had no kids and no real husband to speak of. Albie never accompanied Phylis to the pub, or to any of the local functions for that matter, because his night baking routine six nights a week kept him from going anywhere or joining anything. His only real contact with the human race was with the delivery-van drivers and the few hours he spent at home with his wife when they were both awake.

Poor old Albie, was the general consensus around the township, he was the only one who didn't seem to know what his missus was getting up to while he sweated out his life in the bakery. About as lively and easily rolled as his own bread dough was poor old Albie. But what could anyone do about it? Who was game enough to dob in the local constabulary? No one, it seemed.

However, as is often the case in country towns, things were a little more complex than outwardly showed, for the real truth of the matter was that Albie was a much more astute and solicitous husband than others gave him credit for. He knew full well that his marriage had always been a delicately balanced affair. But would it have improved things if he had hired someone to help him with the baking? He felt not. It was all a bit too late for that.

It wasn't as if their marriage had ever been a romantic affair anyway. It had always been more a matter of convenience. They had in fact married in haste at a very young age when Phylis had thought she was pregnant and didn't dare go to the local quack to confirm it. It was quite a surprise to them both when some weeks later her periods suddenly reverted to normal, and some time after that they both began to realise they had nothing in common other than the bakery. Thus, the smooth running of their business became the prime motivation for their staying together, the arrangement being that neither would interfere with the other unless it threatened their livelihood.

Albie had always worked nights, and you could say his mental clock was set differently from most. Right from the start when he was apprenticed to the local baker at the age of fourteen he'd worked nights. And then, later, when his boss had retired and Albie had bought him out he had chosen to go on working nights. In fact, if anyone had ever bothered to ask him, he would have confessed that he not only preferred the night to the day, he celebrated it. Albie always considered that things were softer at night, more mellow, more mysterious. There was no glare or sharp edges at night and his ear seemed more attuned to the cold isolated sounds of the late night milk train, the echoes of barking dogs and the euphonic croakings of bullfrogs, rather than the ever-present daytime clamour.

And, being a night-bird like the owl, his knowledge of the world was mostly viewed from a nocturnal perspective. He knew the moon and stars more than he knew the sun. He knew when the moon was on the wane or coming on full, even at what time of the night each star constellation was visible. Dull he may have seemed to others in the town but not to himself. Not inside his head, anyway, where he thought of himself as a bit of a loner, a wild card, a vagabond and an explorer. His heart may have seemed to beat a little slower than others but in his own mind he knew, in some things at least, it beat with a great deal more force than anyone else he knew in Montvale.

Once the loaves, buns and pies were in the ovens each night it had become his habit to climb up to the old grain loft on top of the bakery where he would settle himself on the small balcony smoking his pipe and gazing up into the heavens. Such amazements there were. Such mysteries and immensity. He was even convinced he'd seen Sputnik one night, a pinprick of light, wavering its way through the stars from east to west.

It seemed natural enough that his next step was to buy a telescope, through which he could gaze deeper into that magical firmament. To fully accomplish his desire he had arranged with Harvey Stone, the town's carpenter, to convert the old loft into a small observatory with a sliding roof panel, a central platform and glass all around. Every clear night, in between each batch of baking bread, it was his practice to climb the stairs, unwrap the protective sheet covering the scope, slide open the roof panel and peer upwards into the speckled mass of the near universe so he could bring those glittering specks of light into sharp focus, seeing them eventually as separate circular bodies that wheeled through space just like the planet under his feet. Hardly a night passed when he didn't discover something new, something to almost take his breath away.

But Albie's love for the night didn't only run to the heavenly constellations, because he'd found long ago that on those nights unsuitable for star-gazing he could, from his vantage point, also do a bit of town-gazing. Through the evidence of his own eyes Albie had long ago found that, unlike the stars which you could always depend on, the same couldn't be said of many of his fellow citizens.

Under the cloak of darkness, care and respectability seemed not so urgent as they were in the full light of day. He certainly knew quite a bit about the sergeant's after dark activities. More than once he'd focused the scope on the police station and seen the policeman emerge with flashlight and leather riding crop to maraud around the town's side streets, along the river bank and around the back of the pub where any unauthorised stop-outs or wayward younger fry might still be lingering with intent of one kind or another. Albie even knew the exact spot in the rockery where the sergeant hid his backdoor key.

All this was of little interest to Albie until one night he tracked the sergeant in a somewhat different direction. This time through the shadows of the willows along the river bank into Albie's own street, into his own back garden, to his own back door and the welcoming beckon of his own wife. The flaky images in the night lens were even clear enough for Albie to identify the white paper bundle the sarge had tucked under his arm and the brown paper bag poking out of his jacket pocket. A nice brown trout or a rabbit in the butcher's paper, a bottle of brandy or scotch in the pocket.

Over the years he had witnessed many of his wife's indiscretions without rancour - a traveller lingering on in the town when he should have been well gone by the day before, or perhaps a forestry worker who had lived away from home too long, and who found out that Phylis' shop banter and flirtatiousness could lead to something a little more exciting than an extra cream bun in his lunch order.

In the past these clandestine affairs hadn't really worried Albie, but after he witnessed the sergeant's increasing number of calls on his wife he became a little uneasy.

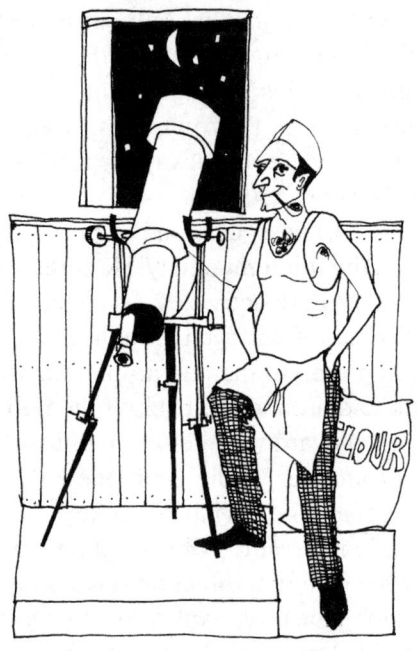

... then as often happens with night workers and stargazers...the answer just came to him.

He didn't like the sergeant much, he considered him to be a lazy sod inclined to turn a blind eye on too much. Many were the times when Albie had brought his scope to bear on the sergeant breaking the very laws he was meant to uphold - getting slipped the odd bottle of scotch from the publican for ignoring pub closing times, for instance, or burning the incriminating feathers of an out-of-season wild duck in the incinerator at the bottom of the station garden. Once he'd even seen that rogue Rolly Hills delivering a large cut of beef carcass through the station backdoor. Only slight misdemeanours maybe, but they revealed to Albie a particular lack of moral fibre. Neither was the sarge just passing through like most of the others. It was a situation that could only come to a bad end, and Albie, loyal and watchful husband that he really was, determined to do something about it, though exactly what, he hadn't a clue.

But then, as often happens with night workers and stargazers, on the Thursday before the night of the Warden's Ball, the answer just came to him. He was just readying himself for his night's foray through the stars when, much to his delight, he saw framed in the patch of night sky to the south the pulsing red heart and curling constellation of Scorpio - his own zodiac sign. So bright and clear it was, his naked eye could trace out the imaginary lines that joined the stars into the shape of a scorpion. And he could have sworn the tail pointed directly down to the police station on the other side of town.

No less excited than Archimedes could have been on discovering the fundamental law of hydrostatics, Albie suddenly shouted over the sounds of the rumbling dough-mixing machines below, "Eureka, that's it!" The scorpion in the sky had given him an idea how he could get rid of the sergeant for good. He hastily covered his telescope and returned to the bakery, where for the rest of the night he planned the details of his revenge...

The town's community hall was a rickety wooden building at the back of the R.S.L. Club. It was used mostly for dances and wedding receptions, although bingo nights and billiard tournaments were sometimes held there in the warmer months. The fact was, the electric wiring in the old building was old and too dangerous to run adequate heating. There was even some talk from time to time about demolition on the grounds of public safety, but the townspeople threatened insurrection if such a thing was attempted. So what if it did sway a little in a strong wind? What if the supper room floor had gaps wide enough for the rats to crawl through? The dance floor itself was sound, after all, and who wanted heating in a dance hall anyway?

So, for more years than anyone cared to remember, there was a weekly dance in the hall. Each Saturday night, winter and summer, the hall throbbed and trembled under the feet of the dancers. Old time, new time, any kind of time was the way the dances proceeded, catering for all tastes and all ages. Free-range kids plummeted in all directions and even the occasional dog had been known to engage in the light-hearted frenzy.

There were those more formal occasions, too, such as the yearly Warden's Invitation Ball when, on the Friday night before the usual Saturday dance, those in the district so inclined could parade their self-styled importance before the ordinary townspeople and pretend they were something special. On that night it was strictly long dresses for the ladies and blue suits and ties for the gents. Only the older school children, dressed in appropriate clothes, were allowed in. There certainly weren't any dogs or babies asleep in porches and changing rooms at the Warden's Invitation Ball.

"They'll all be too busy tryin' to impress each other to have a good time," was the general summing up of those who cared enough to watch the subdued arrival of the participants in the main street earlier.

"Not an honest-to-God smile amongst them," the bookmaker's wife observed to her husband as she peered down from her second storey window.

Though to be fair, the gravity of the graziers wasn't all that surprising. The prices of both wool and grain were down that year and there wasn't much to smile about. Isn't it true that it's the price of a grazier's dag-wool that measures his seasonal smile? It was only when suppertime came around that a marked cheering-up took place, time for the men to talk about their hard-luck prices with fellow sufferers and the women to talk of their current pet charity and why they had given up the one they supported last year. And of course, most of all, it was time for the Warden to make his yearly speech which, given a few slight updates, was exactly the same one he'd been making since he was elected Warden nine years before.

In fact, it was during the Warden's boring speech that his good wife first became aware of something nasty wriggling and poking under her ankle-length frock. Not surprisingly she let out a loud scream and leapt fully two feet sideways, pointing down with a trembling, accusing finger at the crack in the floorboards where, for a brief second before it retreated back through the hole in the floor, a shiny black wriggling thing was visible to all.

At that point someone cried 'Snake!' and it was the signal for panic. Some of the women climbed up onto chairs, flapping their dresses vigorously, as if they too might have found something slithering in their petticoats. Others ran for the nearest door, only to change their minds at the last minute and turn back, colliding into those pushing up behind. Nobody, it seemed, wanted to be the first to leave the hall. Who knew, there might be other beady-eyed nocturnals out there in the dark just waiting to dive on the first bare ankle that stepped through the door. Neither did any of the dancers want to remain in the hall where more of the slippery things might emerge through the cracks in the floorboards. Everyone wanted to escape but nobody knew where escape was. You could say chaos reigned.

Some of the braver male ex-revellers eventually decided the only thing to do was to investigate the foundations under the hall. Time for serious business now. They tucked their socks into their trousers and set about confiscating all available pocket torches. They sacked the billiard room for billiard cues and marched resolutely out through the main exit doors. After much stumbling about through low-lying blackberry bushes and rabbit holes, they finally managed to surround the building. No-one really knew what they would find down there amongst the dry dust and cobwebs, poking this way and that, the lights of their torches confusing with the light coming from the gaps in the floor. It was all a bit weird. They could have expected to find anything.

Anything, that was, except what they did find. There, lying in the dirt amongst the scrabble marks of a hasty and dusty retreat, the torch beams had picked out the abandoned paraphernalia of the alleged culprit. Nothing very terrifying at all really - a regulation issue torch, a policeman's peaked cap and a black riding-crop. The crop itself looked decidedly like the same leathery thing that had tickled around the lady Warden's legs.

Sergeant Tom denied he knew anything about it, of course. He said at the time he'd been out on an urgent call chasing some will-o'-the-wisp accident down the main road ... an urgent late night phone call ... a hoarse muffled voice at the other end of a public phone pleading for help. But the facts spoke for themselves. There was no sign of any accident the following morning, and certainly no public phone to ring from. And although no-one of a sober mind really believed he would be stupid enough to do such a thing, Sergeant Tom Plaister nevertheless felt his authority in the district had been somewhat diminished by the night's fiasco. When his wife returned from New Zealand two weeks later he applied for a transfer back to the city. "Where the crims are more easily identified," were his departing words to Montvale.

Not a bad thing really, the town gossips reasoned, when they heard he'd gone. No need for Albie to find out about it now. Poor old "head in the stars" Albie. Such an innocent as he. How could he have coped with such earthly infidelity?

Dear Editor

Howard Round was the editor of the local weekly newspaper. He had arrived in Montvale township several years back and rented a small room at the back of Conolly's pub. Not long after his arrival he bought an ancient printing press from a friend of his in the city and set up the district's first newspaper in a couple of vacant rooms above the hardware shop in the main street.

From the word go the paper was a great success. For the first time ever the local residents could read about themselves and the events of the district. Their very own paper, reporting in detail about the local footy or cricket, who kicked what goal and who bowled who out, who had won what at the annual agricultural show, who was getting married and who had died.

As time progressed Howard also added columns of more esoteric interests, like local council notes, astrological forecasts, veterinary advice, health advice from the District Nurse, a Dear Dorothy column (humorous rather than serious), a crossword, and notes on the history of settlement by a local amateur historian.

It was all there, week by week, without a miss. There was very little news about the outside world contained in Howard's paper because that could be got from the big daily papers if necessary. The only controversial things about the paper were Howard's editorials which, to the residents' delight, more often than not tore strips off the nepotist inclinations of the municipal councillors.

Where Howard Round had come from, and why such an obviously educated man as he had chosen to settle in their particular neck of the woods, was a mystery and a constant talking point with the locals. Some people suggested that he was hiding from the law, and others, less inclined to drama, that he might have been escaping from family problems. Others (more accurately as it turned out) surmised that Howard may have simply wanted an easy life. Running his paper didn't seem to take much of his time or energy, so consequently he could indulge in his favourite pastime of drinking and talking on any conceivable subject that took his fancy.

Howard himself contributed very little about the circumstances of his past, though he once told Pat the barman at Conolly's pub that those who considered he had run away from something and taken to drink to drown his sorrows were quite wrong. He told Pat that the reverse was true, that he had moved to the country because of two quite specific reasons: one, that drunks were more tolerated in the country, and two, because the living was cheaper. He winked at Pat then, with the kind of wink that neither supported nor denied the truth of his statement, and continued his explanation with just the tiniest of smiles that offered no more hope of drawing a conclusion than his wink had. "More money left over then to indulge my primary obsession," he said as he pushed his empty glass across for a refill.

That same day Howard also revealed that he had been a senior journalist on a city paper and he'd got the sack from that august rag when he punched his editor on the nose during a slight altercation over political policy. "I was intoxicated then, and hallelujah, I am still intoxicated," he told Pat. "The only difference is, here I drink in celebration of my happy state."

"Yer never know whether he's jokin' or serious," Pat told his friends later that evening when Howard had staggered off to his room. So, in spite of the fact Howard was inclined to quote poetry and wax eloquent about many things that his various drinking companions hardly understood, this inclination to be a bit "sissy" was balanced out by the knowledge that here was a bloke man enough to sacrifice his career for the enviable pleasure of thumping the boss on the nose.

Besides, as it turned out, Howard knew as much about horse racing, cricket and football as the best of them. His sports page, according to the locals, was even better than the city daily. The only problem was, when Howard was drunk (which was often) he was inclined to switch his conversation from sports to politics to poetry and back again without warning, so that by mid-afternoon his conversation had become somewhat garbled. Those who wanted to talk seriously with Howard learned to do so before lunch, and as the day progressed they left him alone.

About five o'clock in the afternoon the editor would stagger off to his room and shut himself away. Shortly after, the sound of symphonic music would burst forth from the room and continue unabated until it was pub closing time, when it would just as suddenly cease. When the bar opened the following morning, in would stroll Howard, surprisingly bright and breezy, to begin the whole process over again.

"Dunno how he does it," Pat often observed. "He lives on pies, potato chips and whisky, yet he's never sick. I reckon he's got the constitution of an ox. He told me once he gets up every mornin' before six to do the paper. He must work with a continuous hangover."

But, as eccentric as Howard's behaviour was, the locals came to accept him as a permanent fixture in the town. They certainly accepted his paper which, geared to their needs, gave them a greater sense of community. "That Howard's a bit strange but he's okay," seemed to be the general consensus amongst the locals.

The only person who never really accepted Howard was Colonel Foote, shire councillor and self-proclaimed gentleman farmer. Curiously enough the Colonel was also an outsider, having bought land in the district in the early fifties when he had retired from the army. However, because he had bought the largest property in the district and was a relatively rich man, the Colonel was inclined to assume an outsized sense of his own importance. Such an attitude might have fooled some of the less thoughtful locals but it certainly didn't fool Howard, who knew that a well-modulated speaking voice had little to do with intelligence or personal worth.

Thus, having sussed the Colonel out for being a blustering fool, Howard took much delight in sending him up at every opportunity. The Colonel, naturally enough, resented this challenge to his previously undisputed role as patron and benefactor of the district. Before Howard had arrived with his "silly little paper" nobody dared criticise his actions - not to his face anyway - and, according to the Colonel, nobody, especially not a down-and-out drunk, was going to do it now.

The feud between the two simmered away for several years, either by the printed word in Howard's paper, or by verbal quip whenever the opportunity arose. Unfortunately for the Colonel, his past army background and his present self-proclaimed lord of the manor status, didn't guarantee him the benefit of a quick wit. The Colonel was used to giving unequivocal orders that were to be acted upon without question. Argumentation was foreign to him, as was rational discussion. He was no match for Howard who had spent his apprenticeship defending his opinion every step of the way. It wasn't too surprising that the journalist, drunk or otherwise, always managed to have the final say. This infuriated the Colonel no end and he became more and more antagonistic towards Howard. Both his verbal attacks and his letters to the editor took on an increasingly vitriolic and irrational tone.

"There's nothin' those two can agree on," Pat idly remarked one evening to a small group of pub patrons, "except perhaps their likin' for the booze. Howard attacks whisky like he's got shares in half a dozen Scottish distilleries and is tryin' to keep their profits up ... an' the Colonel's not far behind. The only difference is Howard shouts his drinkin' problem from the roof tops an' the Colonel does his drinkin' in private." He gave a knowing wink across the bar. "Both of them's been warned off it by the quack, I hear."

It was inevitable the feud would spill over one day, and that it did! During the height of the Vietnam controversy the Colonel, who was the President of the local R.S.L., made a speech on ANZAC day which seem to eulogise the war. In the following edition of his paper Howard got stuck into the Colonel with his usual wit and sarcasm. He called the local R.S.L. "a war-struck band of decrepit and dishevelled Gilbert and Sullivan major-generals rattling their rusty cutlasses at imaginary enemies."

The Colonel, of course, was incensed. Against his usual practise he made a personal appearance in the public bar of Conolly's hotel the day after Howard's editorial appeared and in a loud authoritative voice ordered himself a whisky. Howard, who was slumped in his favourite stool at the corner of the bar, caught the Colonel's eye and gave him a huge wink.

The Colonel's usually red face took on an almost crimson hue, and the few drinkers present who quickly sized up the situation waited breathlessly for the inevitable onslaught. However, the Colonel said nothing, he simply tossed his whisky down and ordered a second.

"... he gets up every mornin' before six to do the paper. He must work with a continuous hangover."

Eventually it was Howard who began the duel. "Hi, major-general," he said thickly. "Did you like my editorial?"

The Colonel appeared to ignore the question. He stared steadfastly to the front for a few seconds and when he did finally speak, rather than direct his words to Howard as everyone had expected him to, he addressed them to Donny Conolly behind the bar. "You know, Mr Conolly," he said slowly and carefully, "it's easy for those who haven't had to fight a war to criticise, but as you well know it was the so-called major-generals who stopped this country being overrun by the yellow peril in forty-four. Though when I come to look around at this country these days, I sometimes wonder whether it was worth the sacrifice."

The drinkers present automatically turned their heads towards Howard as if waiting for his caustic rejoinder. Unfortunately it was three o'clock in the afternoon. Howard was well below his best. He merely mumbled something about burying Caesar, and the Colonel, having taken stock of the rather pathetic slump of Howard's shoulders, seemed suddenly to grasp something he hadn't been aware of before. His face took on a distinctly predatory expression as he addressed his next words to nobody in particular. "As a professional soldier I always held the view that there were two kinds of blokes who were a liability in any company of mine - the first was a commie-lover who hadn't the heart for a good fight, and the second, to put it bluntly, was a poofter you couldn't turn your back on. It is my opinion that if one happens to be both then the best thing to do with him would be to shoot the poor bastard and put him out of his misery."

The locals were used to the Colonel's bluster but this last thrust was beyond their experience. They began shuffling uncomfortably as they waited for Howard to lift the tone of the verbal battle to something more like its usual level. Howard, however, seemed incapable of reply. He just swayed a little on his stool before he lifted his glass and drained it. Then, with as much dignity as he could muster, he slid off the seat and walked rather hesitantly towards the guests' door, mumbling something that nobody present could quite catch. The triumphant Colonel Foote raised his own glass in the direction of Howard's departing figure and drained his whisky with a flourish. Then he replaced the empty glass on the counter and marched out of the pub...

"Don't you worry," Pat said later when he heard the story. "Howard'll get him back - just wait an' see if he don't."

Many others agreed, but nobody could have predicted the extraordinary circumstances in which this would come about. As it happened it was the last argument anyone would witness between Howard and the Colonel because the following week the Colonel suffered a severe stroke and within a month he was dead. The funeral was about the biggest the district could ever remember, a small town equivalent to a full state funeral. Though it must also be said that there were few who shed any tears.

As editor of the local paper it was up to Howard to write the Colonel's obituary. The townspeople waited with some interest to see how Howard would handle it. They knew him by now as a man with considerable experience but it seemed that whatever Howard did it was going to be the wrong thing. If he said something nasty about the Colonel it would show him up as being mean-minded, and if he said nice things about the Colonel it would inevitably smack of hypocrisy.

With the next issue of Howard's paper it seemed as though Howard had taken the latter course - there was a whole column of it - a eulogy of sorts that told of the Colonel's history as a soldier and a farmer of some substance. There seemed nothing that anyone could possibly quarrel with. Except, perhaps, that it made the Colonel out to be even more of an identity than he really was.

Until, that was, Amy Pike, who was the proprietor of the local sweet shop and a more astute reader than most, discovered what she took to be a misprint. When referring to the wartime exploits of the Colonel, instead of reading 'this battle-scarred warrior' it read 'this battle-scared warrior'.

Howard, of course, had to acknowledge the error in his following edition, but again it seemed the eccentricities of his ancient printing press had the final say about the Colonel. The apology read: "In last week's edition there was a misprint in the obituary of the late Colonel Foote. The phrase 'battle-scared warrior' should, of course, have read 'bottle-scarred warrior'. For that unforgivable error we sincerely apologise."

Nobody mentioned the second misprint as such but the rumour was that Howard had been shouted several free drinks that day. And later when the bar was closed Pat the barman, who had carried a rather smug "I told you so" expression around all day, stuck both the article itself and the apology up on the pub noticeboard before he went home - the pertinent phrases underlined in black.

If you're ever passing through Montvale district and drop into Conolly's pub for a quick drink you'll probably find they're still there...

Bert Morley's Killing

Bert Morley was a travelling salesman who had been making seasonal trips to the district in his mobile shopper for nearly twenty years. His lines ran to needles, threads, balls of wool, pins, soft fabrics, sewing boxes and clothing. Given the chance he could even conjure up the very latest of sewing machines from under the counter and run a demo on the spot.

"This machine," he'd say to the envious wives, "will save you many an hour and bleedin' finger. This machine will buttonhole and embroider to your heart's content; it will darn hubby's socks for you and fancy stitch his underpants like you wouldn't believe. This little machine will turn your lives around ladies; you just see if it doesn't."

In his late fifties, Bert was a lugubrious man whose expression rarely changed. His manner was gloomy and his speaking voice without any inflection whatsoever. Consequently, when he spoke, he seemed always to be complaining about something, even if he wasn't. His slight figure, inevitably clothed in a dark blue, double-breasted, pin-striped suit with plain red tie to match, was permanently stooped, as if he carried the woes of the world on his narrow shoulders.

Phylis Barnes from the bakery always reckoned that Bert's personality was more suited to the undertaking profession than the sales profession. "Even when he tells a joke it comes out more as a lament," she said. "Whenever he comes into my shop to buy his meat pies I feel depressed for the rest of the day."

Certainly Bert's words alone wouldn't have convinced anybody but the most gullible of buyers to take one of his machines but as he talked he also sewed. You could hardly see his hands they darted so fast from here to there - turning knobs, switching stitches, manoeuvring the piece of material this way and that as patterns emerged almost magically from the plain cloth. His slow voice and the quick whirr of the machine created a contrapuntal effect that was almost hypnotic. It was said by many that he was the best little sewer in the district, and that he could get that machine to do damn near everything but sit up and bark.

... his profit margin was low and his costs were rising every year

Bert drove an old Ford bus which he'd had converted into a combination livable caravan and mobile showroom. All the seats had been removed and lines of cupboards were built along each side of a central aisle. The cupboards were so hinged they opened up and out in steps for easy access. At the bottom of one row of cupboards he had a bed which he could wheel in and out with the minimum of fuss, and just back from the front exit door there was a small kitchen space which, during business hours, converted to a counter for charging and wrapping.

Bert's customers entered the bus from the back end and made their way through his lines of goods to the front door. All in all it was a very efficient self-serve system that suited Bert and his customers alike. And because his overhead costs were less than the local shopkeepers his prices were very competitive. Business was brisk from the moment he arrived and set up his bus in the main street until the time he packed up ready to move on to the next town.

The local shopkeepers didn't much like Bert taking their business away. Whenever he was in town they were forever grumbling about money leaving the District, but, other than grumble, there wasn't much they could do about it because Bert always made sure his current hawker's licence was prominently displayed in the front window of his bus.

However, in spite of running a profitable little business, Bert was often heard to confess he got a bit sick of always being on the move, and that one day he intended to retire with his long-suffering wife to a little cottage by the sea he'd had his eye on for quite a while.

"I'd do nothing then but grow vegetables out the back, read the papers and stare out the window at the sea. All I need is a couple a thousand more of these," he'd say as he shoved their banknotes into his ancient metal till. He would try for a smile then, as if he were only joking. But it was a sad affair; it could have been mistaken for a smirk.

Whenever he mentioned the subject of his retirement Bert was inclined to go off into a kind of thoughtful reverie, as if at that very moment he was looking out his dream cottage window counting the bean rows. Then he would suddenly give a bit of a start sigh heavily and continue wrapping the package of goods he had before him.

Though, according to Phylis Barnes who considered herself an expert on Bert Morley, it could have been a simple bit of revery he was indulging himself in, or then again it could be a touch of epilepsy, a petit mal like her cousin. After all, he was the same, sad, washed-out skinny type.

But, for all the enthusiasm displayed by the local ladies to buy Bert's wares, retirement still seemed a long way off because the cold hard fact was his profit margin was low and his costs were rising every year. What he really longed for was something special to sell - something that he could really get his teeth into. A sale line with such potential he could make a quick killing and finally realise his dream of retirement. Though what that could be he had no idea.

That was until on one such trip to the district he found a letter waiting for him at the town's post office. It was from an acquaintance of his who worked for a clothing warehouse, offering him, the letter said, the chance of a lifetime - five hundred ladies' frocks at less than half cost price. "The frocks are excellent quality," his acquaintance wrote. "The only problem is they are last year's fashion, something I thought wouldn't particularly worry your country clientele - all sizes are available."

Back in his bus that night Bert re-read the letter for the umpteenth time and with his pencil began jotting down a reasonably optimistic cost and profit estimate of how much money he could make if he sold out the frocks at slightly above wholesale rates, a price most of his customers couldn't refuse. The total he came to was considerable. It certainly seemed as though his ship had come in - if he could sell the majority of the frocks at such a price that little cottage by the sea he so longed for would be within his reach.

He decided he would ring his acquaintance and accept his offer the very next day. In anticipation he wrote out his cheque and put it in an envelope ready for mailing. He was so excited by the prospect of his windfall he didn't get to sleep until it was almost morning and when he did his dreams were crowded with images: rows and rows of green vegetables, trailing vines, garden gnomes, the soft humming of bees, of soaring birds too and the gentle thudding of surf on sand - which was in fact the bakery's machinery across the road kneading the dough for the early morning bread baking. But that was of no importance to Bert, who dreamed on. And if anyone who knew him could have seen his sleeping face that morning, they would have been surprised by his broad and contented smile.

On his return to the district a week later Bert picked up the assignment of frocks from the railway station. Later in his bus he unpacked the boxes with trembling fingers. Would this windfall be as good as he expected? Sure enough, as his acquaintance had promised, the frocks were of excellent style and quality, the first carton a rich blue with white polka dots. He opened the second carton: another twenty blue and white frocks lay folded in their soft tissue paper bedding. The third box was exactly the same. A slow realisation began to dawn. In rising panic Bert began to rip open all the cartons and his terrible suspicion was finally confirmed. Except for the variation of sizes each carton was a duplicate of the first. Five hundred blue frocks with white polka dots! "The bastard," he moaned over and over. "The bastard's sold me a left-over, factory job-lot."

As he drove back to the caravan park he pondered the calamity. How in the blazes was he going to sell five hundred identical frocks in a close-knit community? Even if he toured the entire countryside of his area he'd be unlikely to sell more than half a dozen of the same style frock in any town, no matter how low the price. He broke out in a sweat just thinking about it. Gone was his chance for early retirement. And when his wife found out what he had done she'd most likely kill him. His pleasant dream of the week previous was already turning into a nightmare.

That night, for the first time the locals could recall, the frugal hawker turned up in Conolly's public bar and set about getting roaring drunk. He lined up six beers on the counter and by the time he got to drinking the last beer it hardly had time to go flat.

One of the locals who was even more intoxicated than Bert, sidled up to him and offered to shake his hand. "Good on yer," the man said, "yer a real boozer after all. Have a drink on me to help me celebrate me latest winnin's. Five times in a row now I've taken them bookies to the cleaners."

Already suffering the beginnings of a hangover Bert waved the suggestion away with a weary hand. "Not me, mate, I've got nothing to celebrate. I've got to be up early in the morning, I've got a lot of ground to cover to make up for what I've losht this week."

The man looked a little disappointed. "That's a real shame, that is - for a man to lose his money ... a real shame. We boozers got to stick together after all - there ain't many of us left yer know. Tell yer what, if you're still aroun' next Friday evenin' I could put yer on to two or three real good starters for the local trots on Saturday. What do yer reckon?"

Bert stared back at the man for several seconds. In the turmoil of his recent disaster he had forgotten about the local trots, which apart from show day and the footy finals, was the biggest event on the district's calendar. Even in his hazy and inebriated state he thought he could see a faint glimmer of hope. "The races, ay?" he said finally. Then, with more enthusiasm than he'd had all week, he suddenly reached and grabbed hold of the man's hand and shook it vigorously. "Too bloody right I'll be here. I wouldn't mish it for quids. I'll see you right here nexsht Friday night." With one vague wave in his new friend's direction Bert staggered out of the pub and into the night, a diabolical plan already beginning to form in his addled mind...

To cut a long story short - come race day the weather was perfect. A record crowd turned up. The only thing that marred the proceedings was the embarrassment and suppressed wrath of several hundred or so of the local ladies, of all shapes and sizes, tentatively sporting what was, according to Bert Morley who had showed up unexpectedly on their doorstep during the week previous, the very latest, top quality, blue and white fashion frock of exclusive design that he'd kept especially for them, his favourite customer.

Phylis Barnes, one of those unfortunates cringing from public view in the packed ladies' retiring room that afternoon, was heard to express the general sentiments of her fellow sufferers. "No wonder the miserable little bugger suggested I kept it a secret. What a surprise you'll be on race day, he said. I swear, if he ever shows his face in this district again, he'll be the one who gets the surprise - I'll have his nuts for a necklace."

Something, incidentally, which wasn't likely to happen seeing the word was out that a week or two after race-day Bert had sold up his business and disappeared from view. Probably to that little cottage by the sea he'd had his eye on for so long. What with the price he got for his business, the twenty bucks profit he'd made on each of those frocks, and the doubles' winnings his new found mate Kev Parker had placed for him that day, he could afford to.

Other titles available in the series *Writers of the Huon*:

long swell of passing
Wren Fraser

Ceremonies of the Sun and Moon
Chloe Roe

The Hadlee Stories
Geoff Dean

The Aboriginal Astronomy Discovery Centre
Gordon Patston

Trail of Bones and Godstones
Philomena van Rijswijk

Esperance Press
Dover, Tasmania
Australia 7117
Ph (03) 62981552 Fax (03) 62981197